This story is partly set in an English hospital.
To aid yo...
to some of...

A&E (Accident... ...oom

Community n... ...rse
with specialist ... ...ery
of infants.

Health visitor—a nurse trained in preventative
medicine and midwifery, who educates people
caring for dependents, e.g., babies or the elderly.

House officer—a hospital-based trainee doctor;
also known as an intern or resident.

ITU—Intensive Therapy Unit; a hospital department
where intensive care is given to those patients in a
critical condition or after major operations.

Locum—a doctor who temporarily stands in for
another, due to absence or illness.

NHS—National Health Service; the U.K. public health
system, which offers medical and surgical care, and is
funded by taxpayers.

Obstetrician—a medical professional specializing in
the care of women during pregnancy, labor and the
period immediately after the birth.

Consultant—a senior medical professional
specializing in an area of medicine.

Senior registrar—a specialist surgeon or doctor
who is subordinate to a consultant, but senior to
the house officers.

SHO—senior house officer; after registration, a
doctor who continues working in a hospital can
be appointed to this full-time training position.

INTERNATIONAL DOCTORS

They're guaranteed to raise your pulse!

Meet the most eligible medical men in the world, in our ongoing series of stories by popular authors that will make your heart race!

Whether they're saving lives or dealing with desire, our doctors have bedside manners that send temperatures soaring....

Available only from Harlequin Presents®

Sarah Morgan

THE ITALIAN'S PASSIONATE PROPOSAL

INTERNATIONAL
DOCTORS

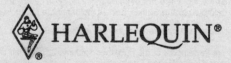

HARLEQUIN®

TORONTO • NEW YORK • LONDON
AMSTERDAM • PARIS • SYDNEY • HAMBURG
STOCKHOLM • ATHENS • TOKYO • MILAN • MADRID
PRAGUE • WARSAW • BUDAPEST • AUCKLAND

ISBN 0-373-12437-6

THE ITALIAN'S PASSIONATE PROPOSAL

First North American Publication 2004.

www.eHarlequin.com

Printed in U.S.A.

CHAPTER ONE

THE freezing air was thick with softly falling snowflakes and the darkened streets of the East End of London were totally deserted. With less than a week to go until Christmas, most people were at home, decorating trees and wrapping presents.

Carlo Santini was barely aware of the inhospitable nature of his surroundings. He was restless and on edge, frustrated beyond belief by recent developments in his life. A frown on his handsome face, he paced rhythmically along the icy pavement, his footsteps muffled by the thick covering of snow, the collar of his black coat turned up against the cold.

He'd been warned to keep to his apartment and the hospital but he was totally fed up with the warnings.

In fact, he was so disillusioned with his life that when things had finally come to a head and he'd been ordered to leave Italy for a short time, he'd been only too happy to comply.

His old life was starting to feel like a prison.

Having enormous wealth was a fantasy for most people but for Carlo the reality had become an increasing burden over the years and he embraced the chance to pretend that it didn't exist, even for a few precious weeks. Being forced to come to London and work under an assumed name was a gift that he was determined to grab with both hands.

For the first time in his whole life, no one would know who he was.

People would respond to his medical and personal skills

rather than his reputation as a billionaire playboy or his impressive connections.

Suddenly aware of just how quiet the streets were, Carlo narrowed his eyes and took a brief look around. He'd always refused to have a personal bodyguard and the recent threats to his life hadn't changed that. He preferred to look out for himself.

He gave a slight smile. Matteo Parini, his father's chief of security, was probably in their London apartment biting his nails at this very moment, wondering where he was.

And Carlo was under no illusions about his safety. Even hidden in the East End of London under an assumed name, he wasn't safe. Not until they caught the men who were threatening his life. But at least for a few hours he could pretend that nothing was wrong.

Suddenly aware that two men had appeared in the street ahead of him, he tensed his broad shoulders slightly. They were walking slowly and Carlo's eyes narrowed suspiciously as he watched them.

Why would they be dawdling when it was below freezing? It was hardly the night for a winter stroll.

Then he saw one of them glance across the street and for the first time noticed a young boy, slight in build, hurrying along the pavement, clutching a stuffed bin bag, his eyes down as he struggled against the snow.

Guessing their intention before they'd even acted, Carlo removed his hands from his pockets, his lean features suddenly showing a strength of purpose. Without drawing attention to himself, he increased his pace, every sense on alert as he closed the distance between them.

With no warning they suddenly turned and sprinted across the snowy street, attacking the young boy viciously, grabbing the bin bag that he was carrying and pushing him roughly to the ground.

Carlo's eyes gleamed and adrenaline rushed through his

veins, but before he could reach them the young boy was back on his feet, lithe and agile. He grabbed one of the men in a classic judo hold and threw him heavily onto the pavement.

Carlo winced at the sickening thud and gave a surprised smile.

Maybe the lad didn't need his help after all. He seemed to be doing pretty well by himself.

Or maybe not...

As the man lay groaning on the ground, his accomplice grabbed the boy round the throat and Carlo saw a flash of steel.

His blood heating, he moved swiftly, using the element of surprise to his advantage, attacking the man from behind and enclosing his wrist in a deadly grip until the knife fell to the ground.

'Let him go...' He couldn't think of a suitable word in English so he switched to Italian, twisting the man's arm behind his back in a ruthless hold that forced him to release the boy.

The other attacker scrambled to his feet, winded by the fall, bracing himself for a fight.

Breathing heavily, he caught the cold, dangerous look in Carlo's eyes and backed away, his change of heart evident.

'Hey, it wasn't my idea...'

He glared at his friend, still held captive by Carlo's deadly hold, and then turned and ran for it, sprinting away as fast as he could, slipping and sliding on the snowy street in his haste to put distance between them.

Swearing fluently, the other man whimpered with the pain in his arm and Carlo reluctantly let him go, kicking the knife out of reach, cold fury erupting inside him. Why were they attacking a kid?

Rubbing his arm, the man gave an angry snarl, landed

a final vicious kick in the boy's stomach and then turned and ran after his friend.

Carlo was itching to chase them but he was aware that the young boy was doubled up in pain from the kick. He reached out a hand to offer support and found himself flat on his back on the pavement, staring up at the stars.

How the hell had that happened?

He was an expert in several martial arts and had spent his entire life prepared to defend himself. He just hadn't expected to have to defend himself from someone who didn't even reach his chin and whom he'd just rescued.

But clearly the boy didn't realise he was being rescued.

Grunting with pain, every muscle in his body protesting, Carlo struggled to sit up and then ducked as a booted foot flew in the direction of his face.

'Stay away from me, you scum!'

Deciding that this was becoming dangerous, he grabbed the foot and brought the boy down as gently as he could, rolling on top of him so that he could hold him securely.

'I'm not trying to hurt you,' he gritted, grabbing both arms and pinning the boy to the pavement. Finally the boy stopped wriggling and glared up at him defiantly and Carlo felt something shift in his stomach.

He'd never seen a boy with eyes that beautiful.

They were an amazing shade of green, fringed with thick lashes that were inky black.

Following through on a totally male instinct, he released the boy's hands and jerked off the woolly hat, sucking in his breath as soft dark hair tumbled down and trailed in the snow.

Not a boy...

His last coherent thought was that she was the most beautiful girl he'd ever seen in his life.

And then she hit him.

Carlo winced as her small fist made contact with his

cheekbone, pain splitting the side of his face. He swore fluently in Italian and moved his jaw gingerly, testing for fractures.

He'd say this for the girl, she certainly knew how to fight. Why had he ever thought she needed his protection?

Careful not to hurt her, he shifted himself so that he pinned her more securely and caught hold of her hands as she struggled.

'*Porca miseria*, I'm not attacking you,' he growled impatiently. 'I'm rescuing you!'

Her eyes were blazing up into his, her chest rising and falling as she tried to catch her breath.

'Rescuing me? You're not rescuing me, you're suffocating me! And ranting at me in a strange language. Let me go!'

She was gorgeous.

Utterly captivated, Carlo gave her a lazy smile but didn't move an inch. He was enjoying it far too much to move. The feel of her soft, womanly body under his was fantastic. How could he ever have thought she was a boy?

He must be losing it...

Her outraged glare faded and she stared up at him, her stunning green eyes locking with his. 'Are you going to lie on top of me all night?'

Given the chance, yes.

'Is that an invitation?' Carlo knew he ought to move and help her up, but all he wanted to do was bend his head and kiss her.

So he did.

As his mouth came down on hers he hung onto her hands, fully expecting her to take another swipe at him, but after the briefest hesitation her soft lips parted and she kissed him back, sighing slightly as he used all the skill of his thirty-four years to seduce a response from her.

When he finally dragged his mouth away from hers he

felt drugged. It had only been a taste but it had been enough to make him want the whole meal.

'Wh-what did you do that for?' Those amazing green eyes were still staring up at him, and for the first time in his life Carlo found it difficult to string a coherent sentence together. His body and brain felt disconnected.

'Kiss of life,' he murmured huskily, his mind and body still focused on her mouth. 'They were pretty rough with you—I thought maybe...'

'I don't think it worked.' Her expression was slightly dazed and her voice was smoky and feminine. 'Want to try it again?'

Carlo lowered his head and kissed her thoroughly, this time releasing his grip so that he could use his hands to haul her body even closer to his.

He felt her shudder under him, felt her slim arms slide round his neck, and for endless moments he was lost in the soft, sweet wonder of her mouth.

Then he heard a shout from the pavement opposite and rolled to his feet, instantly alert.

Be discreet, his father and brother had said.

Lying on a snowy pavement kissing a gorgeous female in full view of anyone who happened to pass probably didn't qualify, he admitted ruefully, reaching down a hand to pull her up.

She staggered to her feet and then jerked her hand away as if his touch had singed her.

'I can't believe we just did that.' She backed away from him and lifted her fingers to her lips, her expression stunned. 'I can't believe I let you kiss me. You're a stranger. I don't kiss strangers.'

She looked confused and wary, and he forced himself to stand still and give her some space. He could hardly blame her for being nervous of him. After all, she'd just been mugged.

Carlo searched for the words to reassure her, but before he could speak she stooped to pick up the bin bag and winced in pain.

'Are you hurt?' He frowned, surprised and confused by the rush of possessiveness that swamped him. He didn't even know her name, but the thought that they'd hurt her filled him with red-hot anger. 'That was a nasty kick.'

He searched his brain for a non-sexual way of suggesting that he take a look at her stomach. He was a doctor after all.

'I'm OK.' She brushed her snowy dark hair away from her exquisite face. 'I suppose I've got you to thank for that.' She gave him a cautious look, still keeping herself at a safe distance. 'If you hadn't intervened he probably would have used that knife. I'm sorry I floored you. It all happened so fast I panicked. I thought you were with them.'

She still looked wary, and every muscle in her body was tense, but at least she hadn't run off.

'Don't apologise. I'm glad you floored me.' Remembering the feel of her soft body under his, he was more than glad. If she hadn't done that, he probably wouldn't have kissed her. *And, having kissed her...*

His eyes dropped hungrily to her mouth again and he wrestled with the instinct to act like a caveman and drag her somewhere quiet, where he could make love to her until she couldn't stand up.

But she was visibly nervous and he wasn't going to blow his chances by rushing her. So, instead of grabbing her, he pushed his hands firmly into his pockets and kept his distance.

'Do you always kiss people who knock you to the ground?' She was watching him carefully with those incredible eyes, as if she hadn't quite decided whether she should run or not.

'Never.'

Her fingers tightened on the bin bag. 'So why did you kiss *me*, then?'

Carlo was finding it harder and harder to breathe normally. 'Because you're stunning.'

The wariness left her face and she threw back her head and laughed aloud. 'Dressed in torn jeans and an ancient coat with a woollen hat on my head? Very sexy, I'm sure.'

'Kissing is a good way of distracting an attacker,' he drawled, unable to drag his gaze away from her gorgeous face. 'It's the element of surprise.'

'Well, I've done judo since I was six but that's a move I've never used,' she confessed, still smiling. Suddenly she seemed more relaxed. Her eyes sparkled and snow stuck to her lashes and shiny dark hair, and it occurred to him that if he could have anything he wanted for Christmas then it would be her.

Preferably unwrapped.

'Are you saying that you've never been kissed by your opponent before?' His words and eyes teased her but his body and brain were deadly serious as he moved closer. 'You've been missing out.'

Their eyes locked and she smiled hesitantly. 'It certainly takes your mind off fighting.' Suddenly her smile faded and she stared at his cheekbone in dismay. 'Oh, no! Did I do that? Have I given you a black eye?'

He didn't care about his eye. At the moment he was more concerned about other parts of his anatomy that he was finding distinctly uncomfortable. His jeans were just too tight to accommodate such an extreme reaction.

She stood on tiptoe and touched his bruised cheekbone gingerly, her voice contrite. 'We ought to get some ice on that.'

Ice. He gritted his teeth. Maybe if he thought about ice

it would help him out of his dilemma. He was reacting like a hormonal teenager.

He looked down at her. 'Are you sure you're all right? They were pretty rough with you.'

It occurred to him that, apart from being wary of him, she didn't seem particularly shaken up. He tried to think of one other woman of his acquaintance who would have fought like that and still been smiling afterwards. He failed dismally. All the women he knew panicked if they so much as chipped a nail.

'I'm OK, thanks to you. Apart from ripping my favourite jeans. I was thinking about something else or they wouldn't have taken me by surprise.' She peered at his face again, her expression guilty. 'You saved my life and in return I hit you. That never happens in the movies. I should have been sobbing with relief and gratitude, instead of which I may have given you a black eye.'

'I love a dominant woman,' Carlo drawled lightly, and she laughed.

'Next time I'll try not to panic.'

'I'm not surprised you panicked.' His expression was serious. 'But I don't think he would have used the knife.'

He said it to reassure her, in case part of her was still scared. Or maybe it was himself that he was reassuring. The thought of what might have happened if that creep had done what he'd threatened was too horrific to contemplate.

She pulled a face. 'If it hadn't been for you, he probably would.' Her tone was matter-of-fact. 'This area is notorious for muggings and other unsavoury acts. I'm lucky you were passing and bothered to help. Do you think we should call the police?'

Carlo froze. The last thing he needed was to draw attention to himself.

'I think they're long gone,' he said carefully, his expression guarded. 'And I didn't really get a good look at them, did you?'

'No.' She shook her head and he changed the subject neatly.

'What are you doing out on your own on a night like this?'

She altered her grip on the bin bag. 'I'm working.'

Working?

What sort of work required her to walk the streets at ten o'clock at night wearing worn jeans, a woolly hat and carrying a bin liner?

Surely she wasn't...

She looked up at him and started to laugh. 'I wish you could see your face! I can assure you I don't do what you're thinking! Actually, I'm a midwife,' she said, as if it was perfectly obvious to anyone but a complete idiot.

A midwife?

He'd worked with midwives for most of his adult life, but none of them had looked like her.

Carlo tried to ask her something intelligent but all he could see was that gorgeous smile that seemed to take over her whole face. Suddenly his brain and his body seemed to be ruled by a vicious rush of male hormones. He'd dated some of the most beautiful women in the world, but he couldn't remember a single one who had threatened his ability to walk in a straight line. Until now.

'Do all English midwives walk around in the dark, carrying bin liners?'

'I was trying *not* to attract attention,' she confided, and he gave a wry smile.

'I think you need more practice.'

'You might be right.' She looked sorrowfully at her torn jeans. 'They must have thought I had something exciting in my bin bag.'

'And have you?'

'Well, I haven't robbed a bank, if that's what you mean.'
She chuckled and hoisted the bag towards her, twisting the
neck so that the contents were safe. 'Actually, I'm on my
way to see a patient. So, if you're sure your face is all
right, I suppose this is where we say goodbye.'

No way!

'I'll come with you,' he said immediately. 'There's no
way I should be allowed to walk these streets on my own.
It's not safe.'

She looked up at him, her cheeks dimpling. 'You need
my protection?'

'Absolutely.' His voice was husky and he saw her breath
catch in her throat.

'You're at least six foot three and you've got more muscles than I've ever seen on one body,' she pointed out,
appreciation in her eyes as they wandered over his broad
shoulders. 'You tackled those guys without a second
thought and you certainly don't look like a man who's
afraid of much.'

Up until five minutes ago he would have agreed with
her, but since the moment she'd thrown him to the floor
everything had changed.

'I'm afraid of never seeing you again.'

The only sound was the soft whisper of snow as it
floated past her stunned face and settled on the black wool
jacket she was wearing.

When she finally spoke her voice was shaky. 'I suppose
I'm meant to say that you're being ridiculous.'

He stepped closer to her, aware of just how delicate she
was. Suddenly he felt fiercely protective. 'Say it, then.'

She stared up at him and he could see that she'd stopped
breathing. 'I—I can't.' A look of confusion crossed her
face. 'Oh, help! What are you doing to me?'

Their eyes held, the heat and tension between them almost melting the snow.

Without shifting his gaze, Carlo held out a hand, and after endless seconds she stepped towards him and took it.

He pulled her against him and stroked her snowy dark hair away from her face, thinking how beautiful she was.

She stared up at him and he could see her breathing quicken. 'I—This is crazy. I really ought to be going...'

'Me, too. Do you think we should kiss each other goodbye?' He was only a breath away from touching her mouth with his when she dipped her head and gave him a gentle push.

'What is it that you do to me? I don't behave like this! I don't even know you.'

Carlo stared down at her thoughtfully, a warm feeling spreading through his body.

He never met people who didn't know him.

In Italy, everyone knew him. His picture appeared regularly in the newspapers and gossip columns and he hated it. He hated being public property.

But to this girl he was a stranger and it was a totally novel experience.

'Everyone is a stranger the first time you meet them,' he pointed out gently, and she gave him a half-smile that betrayed her confusion.

'That's true, I suppose, but I don't usually kiss men I've only known for five minutes.'

'So I'll hang around until you've known me for longer,' Carlo said, and she rolled her eyes in exasperation.

'Are you always this persistent?'

No. He never usually needed to be. He was one of the richest men in Italy and he was usually the one tactfully keeping women at a distance.

'Look, why don't we go somewhere warm and grab a coffee or something?'

'I can't. At least, not right now.' She glanced at her watch and pulled a face. 'There's somewhere I have to be and I don't want to be too late. It's not the best of places in the middle of the day, but at night it's horrid. I meant to go earlier but I had to stay late at the hospital. I need to go and do my visit and you ought to go home and get some ice on your cheek,' she said, touching it with gentle fingers, guilt in her eyes. 'I'm really, really sorry. I wasn't thinking straight.'

'Forget it.' Carlo gave a lopsided smile, wondering where all his smooth chat-up lines had gone when he needed them. He could think of a dozen things to say to her in Italian but none at all in English. 'Just remind me never to get on the wrong side of you.'

She lifted an arm and pretended to flex her biceps. 'Scary, that's me.'

Carlo looked deep into those green eyes and decided that she definitely was scary, but not for any of the reasons she imagined.

The scariest thing of all was that even though he'd only known her for five minutes, there was no way he was letting this woman out of his sight. Part of him knew that he should walk away from her. He was involved in something nasty and he certainly didn't want her dragged into it. But he wasn't prepared to let her go even for a moment. He was going to see where this led and deal with the consequences later.

'All right, if you won't come with me then I'll have to come with you on your call, and then we can both put ice on my face together.'

As a pick-up line it was novel, but he was past caring.

He was a desperate man.

If she turned and walked away, he'd have to consider kidnapping her.

'You can't come with me on my call.' She clutched the bin bag more tightly. 'It's a professional visit. I can't just take a man I picked up on the street.'

'*I* picked *you* up,' he pointed out, and she rolled her eyes.

'Details. Details.'

He gave a lopsided smile. 'Would it help if I confessed that I'm an obstetrician?'

Her eyes widened in disbelief and she started to laugh.

He frowned at her. 'What's so funny?'

'I'm just trying to imagine any of the obstetricians I know fighting like you did.' She shook her head slightly, still laughing. 'I'm failing dismally. They're all very puny and academic. They'd have trouble wrestling with a microscope.'

He lifted an eyebrow, pretending to be offended. 'You don't think I'm academic?'

'You mean you've got all that muscle *and* a brain?' She batted her eyelids and he grinned appreciatively.

'I certainly have.' He adored her sense of humour. 'So, now do you believe I'm an obstetrician?'

'No.' Her cheeks were rosy from the cold. 'I've worked with loads of obstetricians and none of them look like you.'

Was that good or bad?

'So what's wrong with me?'

Her smile faded and he saw the uncertainty in her eyes, and something else that had a serious effect on the fit of his jeans. 'Oh, there's nothing wrong with you at all. That's what I mean.'

His blood heated and he had to stop himself grabbing her again. 'Well, until you see me in action you're just going to have to take my word for it. So, can I come?'

She tipped her head to one side. 'Well, if you're truly an obstetrician, then tell me where you work.'

'I'm doing a locum job at St Catherine's from tomorrow.'

Using a false surname that only he, his security team

*and the most senior member of the hospital were
aware of.*

Her eyes widened. 'That's spooky! I work there, too.'

Did she, now? That was the best news he'd had for
months.

'Which definitely means I can come on your visit,' he
said smoothly. 'We're colleagues. And after that I'm walking you home and we can heal each other's bruises.'

Her lips parted slightly and he held his breath. If she
said no, he was in big trouble.

'I—I don't know...'

The wary look was back and he gave her a smile that
he hoped was non-threatening.

'Look, I know this was an unconventional meeting, but
you don't need to be scared of me. If I step out of line
you can always black my other eye.'

Maybe he was playing dirty by appealing to her conscience but he didn't care. He wasn't going to let her walk
out of his life.

'All right.' She hauled the bag onto her shoulder and
jerked her head towards a high-rise building in the next
street. 'Come with me to see Kelly and then we'll go back
to my place and sort your face out. It's the least I can do
after having tried to half kill you.'

Resisting the impulse to punch the air in triumph, Carlo
shortened his stride to match hers and followed her up
seemingly endless flight of soulless concrete steps that in-
tersected the flats.

He glanced around with a deepening frown.

No wonder she didn't like coming here at night. The
place was menacing and rough. Definitely not somewhere
to be after dark. Especially for a woman on her own. The
walls were covered in graffiti, there were smashed windows and boarded-up doors and, even this close to
Christmas, there was very little evidence of festive cheer.

The girl came to a halt in front of a door, tugged the woollen hat back on her head and stuffed her hair back underneath it.

'All part of the disguise.' She tossed him a smile that made his whole body ache, and tapped on the door.

'Kelly?' She leaned closer to the door. 'Kelly, it's Zan. Let me in.'

Zan? Carlo blinked in surprise.

What sort of a name was Zan?

He was still trying to work it out when the door jerked open and a burly man stood there.

If ever a man was looking for a fight it was this one, and instinctively Carlo straightened his shoulders and prepared himself for trouble.

What the hell was the girl doing in a place like this? This certainly wasn't his idea of midwifery.

'Hi, Mike.' Zan didn't seem remotely nervous. Instead, she just gave the man the same warm smile she'd used on him earlier and peeped round him into the flat. 'Can I see Kelly? I brought some stuff…'

She jiggled the black bin back temptingly and Mike's face darkened.

'We ain't taking no charity!'

Zan shook her head. 'Of course you're not. It isn't charity,' she said easily, her tone relaxed and friendly. 'Mothers swap clothes all the time. Someone I look after was having a clear-out—I just thought you might find it useful, but I can offer it to someone else if you prefer…'

Mike glowered at her and then opened the door wider. 'And while we're at it Kelly ain't going to hospital, so don't even think about suggesting it.' He looked over her shoulder and his eyes narrowed as they fixed on Carlo. He looked at him man to man, his eyes resting on the width of Carlo's shoulders. 'Who's he?'

Zan opened her mouth but Carlo spoke first.

'I'm a doctor. Carlo Bennett.'

He almost stumbled over the surname, because it wasn't his and he wasn't used to it yet, but it was the name that everyone had agreed he should use while he was hiding out in London. As a qualified surgeon he was actually entitled to call himself Mr, but he didn't think this was the time to worry about the finer points of titles. 'I'm going to be working in this area and Zan said I could come with her on some visits.'

Aware that Zan was staring at him, Carlo gave the other man a friendly smile and reached out a hand.

There was a moment's hesitation and then Mike shook it briefly, but his expression was still unfriendly.

'You don't look English and you don't sound English.'

'Part Italian,' Carlo lied smoothly, denying some of his heritage in the interests of discretion. Mike pulled a face, leaving no one in any doubt of what he thought of foreign doctors.

'Well, you can come in as you're here, but you might as well know that I hate doctors and I'm not having one of them near my woman. Zan's the only one I'll let look at her.'

'No problem.' Careful to be non-confrontational, Carlo strolled into the flat after Zan, trying not to show his shock as they walked into the tiny sitting room.

The room was filthy and stacked high with old newspapers and half-eaten plates of food. In the middle of the carpet a German shepherd dog lay with its head on one paw, eyes fixed warily on Carlo.

The place was damp and freezing, and in the corner was a thin wisp of a girl with a rounded stomach and skinny legs.

'Hi, Kelly.' Clearing a space on the sofa, Zan sat down and opened the bin bag. 'How are you feeling?'

Kelly glanced nervously at Mike, who gave a nod. 'I'm

doing OK,' she said in a low voice, 'but I'm pretty tired. Well, very tired, actually.'

And he would have bet half his fortune that she was anaemic, Carlo thought, running a professional eye over the patient and her surroundings. Judging from the remains of the food on the plate, she wasn't eating properly.

'I think it's possible that you may be anaemic,' Zan was saying as she delved into the bag for a blood-pressure cuff. 'That basically means that your blood isn't carrying enough oxygen. It can happen very easily when you're pregnant, especially if you don't eat properly.'

Carlo blinked with admiration. So she'd homed in on the same problem immediately.

She checked Kelly's blood pressure and then glanced at Mike. 'I really want to take a blood sample, Mike.'

'No way.' His tone was unfriendly. 'I'm not having you sticking needles in her. Just do what you have to do and leave.'

Zan's expression was understanding. 'I'm just trying to help her, Mike. She's thirty-four weeks pregnant. If she is anaemic then that could be the reason she's so tired, and we need to get it sorted out before she has the baby. I want to check the iron levels in her blood.'

'No needles.' Mike moved towards Zan and Carlo took a step forward, ready to intervene.

No way was that thug going any nearer to Zan.

'If you've got iron in your bag then just give it to her,' Carlo said smoothly, and three pairs of eyes turned to look at him.

'There's a strong chance that you are anaemic, and obviously we'd like to check that out.' He spoke directly to Kelly. 'But if you'd rather we didn't then the next best thing is to just give you the iron.'

'Will it hurt the baby?'

'It could hurt you if you don't have it,' Carlo said

gently. 'Being pregnant and giving birth to a child place huge demands on your body. We need to correct it or you could have problems during your delivery and you'll be exhausted afterwards. When you come into the hospital we—'

'She ain't coming into the hospital!' Mike growled, and Zan cleared her throat.

'Don't let's worry about that now. You've got my number, and you know that I'll deliver Kelly any time you want me to, anywhere you want me to, but we really do need her to take some iron.' She reached into her bag and pulled out a bottle of tablets. 'Will you take one a day for me?'

Kelly glanced at Mike for approval before taking the bottle, and he gave a brief nod.

'And now can I just check the position of the baby?'

'Not with him in the room.' Mike glared at Carlo, who strolled towards the living-room door immediately.

'I'll wait in the hallway.'

Whatever had happened to the man to make him so suspicious?

Five minutes later Zan called him back in.

Her eyes were troubled as they met his. 'I don't think the baby is growing quite as fast as it should—She's small for thirty-four weeks.'

Carlo lifted his eyes to Mike. 'Can I examine her?'

'No!'

'Mike, please?' Zan's voice was soft and reassuring and Mike hesitated, his jaw set.

Finally he nodded. 'All right.' He glared at Carlo. 'But I'm watching you.'

'That's fine.' Carlo moved his hands skilfully over the mother's abdomen, thinking that he'd never seen such a half-starved waif in his life. Normally he dealt with the pampered wives of the hideously wealthy, and the contrast was extreme. As he examined the girl he realised just how bored he'd become, working in his world-famous Women's Unit in Milan. The case he was seeing now presented so much more of a challenge, both medically and socially.

'Well?'

Mike was looking at him threateningly and Carlo picked up the tape measure that Zan had used and measured Kelly from the top of the bump to her pelvic bone. The measurement was supposed to correlate roughly to the number of weeks of pregnancy, but in this case Zan was right. The baby seemed small.

'Do you smoke?'

Kelly shook her head, but her eyes slid nervously to Mike and Carlo deduced that the man probably smoked heavily and that she was therefore subjecting the baby to passive smoking.

'The baby does seem slightly smaller than we would like,' he said gently, talking directly to Kelly. 'Ideally I'd like to get you to come to the hospital for a series of scans. Nothing scary. We just slide a clever device that's basically a camera over your stomach and we're able to measure the size of the baby's head. That gives us an indication of what size the baby should be, and we can then take a look at the rest of him.'

Kelly glanced at Mike, who shook his head.

'She's not going to hospital.'

Carlo frowned. 'But—'

'That's fine,' Zan interrupted quickly, shooting Carlo a warning look. 'But if you change your mind then come and see us any time. I brought you some clothes, Kelly.'

She delved into the bin bag again and pulled out another bag full of tiny baby clothes, vests and a gorgeous blanket.

Carlo's eyes narrowed.

If those clothes were second-hand then he was an Englishman.

Kelly gave a gasp and her face suddenly shone like the sun coming out from behind a cloud.

'Someone was giving this away?' She fingered one of the outfits in disbelief and Zan smiled.

'They were no use to her.'

Oh, sure.

'But they're like new.' Kelly looked at Mike, her expression pleading. 'Can I keep them—please?'

Carlo found himself holding his breath and finally Mike nodded. 'I suppose so,' he muttered.

'Oh, and I've had a word with the council,' Zan said casually, 'and they're trying to rehouse you in a flat on the first floor.'

Kelly looked at her with hope in her eyes. 'Really?' Her slim shoulders sagged slightly. 'I just can't let myself get excited in case it doesn't happen.'

'It will happen, Kelly,' Zan said firmly. 'There's no way you can stay here. The weather is getting colder, the flat is damp and there's fourteen flights of stairs between you and the ground floor. How are you going to manage that with a baby when the lift's out of order? I've been talking to Social Services about rehousing you and they're doing their best.'

Carlo listened to her and wondered if the couple had any idea how lucky they were to have Zan to fight their corner.

'She can take the tablets, but she ain't coming to hospital for that scan thing,' Mike said, and Zan looked him in the eye.

'The baby isn't big enough, Mike. We really need to—'

'Get out!'

Kelly flinched and shrank back into her chair.

Carlo's eyes narrowed slightly and he drew himself up to his full height, preparing himself for trouble.

'We're leaving,' Zan said calmly, smiling at Mike as though he hadn't just yelled at her in the rudest way possible. 'We'll talk about it again next time.'

'She ain't going to the hospital and that's final.'

Zan stood up. 'That's fine, Mike.' She turned to look at Kelly, her gaze direct. 'Any problems, call me.'

With that she looked meaningfully at Carlo and walked out of the flat with him following close behind.

CHAPTER TWO

'DOES he hit her?' Carlo followed her down the dark staircase and back onto the streets.

'I don't think so.' Zan turned sharp left and then right down a wide road that stretched along the river. 'I think he's just very controlling.'

'And why does he hate hospitals so much?'

'He's never told me, and I don't push it or I won't get to see Kelly at all.' She glanced sideways and tried not to stare.

She'd never met anyone as strikingly good-looking as Carlo before. Tall, dark-haired and loaded with sex appeal, he exuded a strength and confidence that was magnetic. If she'd had to pick one word to describe him, it would have been *male*. Carlo was very, *very* male.

And he had good shoulders.

She remembered the weight of his body when he'd lain on top of her and smiled slightly. For once she could walk home without worrying.

Who in their right mind would pick a fight with him?

Carlo was frowning. 'Do you have to visit them?'

'Well, if I don't then she gets no antenatal care whatsoever,' Zan told him, crossing over the road so that they could walk next to the river. Fairy lights had been strung between the trees and their reflection danced over the surface of the water. 'Social Services first told me that she was pregnant, but she hasn't seen a doctor once in her whole pregnancy. To start with Mike wouldn't let me in, but I've worked on him and now I get to see her. I'm hoping that if she sees enough of me I'll be able to get her to trust me.'

'She needs a biophysical assessment,' Carlo said, and Zan nodded.

He was referring to an established technique using ultrasound to look at the baby and to measure the heart-rate.

'I know. The truth is she needs a lot of things she isn't getting. It's very worrying, but we can only do the best we can. It's hard enough getting access at all.'

She felt his eyes slide over her. 'Presumably that's why you dress like that? Because they're suspicious of authority?'

He was smart; she'd give him that.

'That's true, but I also hate walking around this area at night,' she confessed. 'I might be a black belt in judo but I'm not stupid. If I have to do it then I dress down and I wear trainers. If anyone suspected I was medical they'd be attacking me for drugs.'

'It isn't a suitable place for a woman to be working.' His gaze darkened ominously and she chuckled.

'Are you always this macho?'

'Of course.' Carlo's arrogant dark head lifted and a wry smile touched his handsome face. 'I'm Italian, remember? Despite our efforts to be politically correct, deep down we still expect our women to stay at home and warm the bed for us.'

The mention of bed brought a faint colour to her cheeks. Whoever warmed his bed would be a *very* lucky woman, but she wasn't telling him that. 'Someone must have forgotten to tell you that this is the twenty-first century.'

He didn't smile, his gaze disturbingly direct. 'It's not a safe area for you to work in.'

He was breathtakingly good-looking and Zan was finding it hard to peel her eyes away from him.

'I work here because it's challenging and I'm really doing some good.' She looked at him curiously. 'This isn't what you're used to, is it? You looked pretty shocked when you saw the flat.'

He pulled a face and rubbed a hand across the back of his neck. 'Was it that obvious?'

'Only to me. Don't worry about it. I was pretty shocked myself when I first came here after twenty years of middle-class upbringing. It's a real eye-opener. Lots of teenage pregnancies, lots of unmarried mothers with several children by different men, and every flat you visit has a German shepherd dog the size of a wolf.' She stepped gingerly over a patch of ice. 'I suppose I'd have one, too, if I lived in this area. The dogs used to be the worst part of the job for me, but generally I've got used to them. Do you have dogs at home?'

He hesitated and then nodded. 'Yes, dogs don't bother me. So, why did you learn judo?'

Zan smiled and huddled more deeply into her coat to keep out the cold. 'I have four older brothers. My father was going for a five-a-side rugby team but then they had me.' She shrugged. 'Anyway, they all decided that I needed to know how to take care of myself just in case they weren't around to do it for me.'

'Sensible.'

'No, massively over-protective,' she said dryly. 'They've scared off every boyfriend I've ever had.'

Carlo looked at her curiously. 'But you're close?'

'I adore them,' she said simply. 'Growing up with four big brothers was just the best thing in the world. We had such fun.'

'But they've taught you to be wary of men?'

She hesitated for a moment and then nodded. 'Yes. Yes, they have. I may love my brothers but I'd hate to be anything other than their baby sister. They're rogues, and when they were growing up they treated women appallingly. I've learned lots about men by watching them. And because they know exactly how men think and act, they scare off anyone male who shows an interest in me.'

'Ouch.' Carlo gave a rueful smile and glanced around him at the dark shadows. 'So can I expect to be pounced on any moment?'

Zan looked at his shoulders and laughed. 'I don't think you've got much to worry about. So, now you know about me, how about you? All I know is that you're part-Italian. What I want to know is, which part?'

He shot her a suggestive smile that was so sexy she almost stopped breathing.

'If you're good, I'll show you later.'

His teasing drawl made her blush, but she couldn't help smiling. There was something so good-humoured and honest about him.

'Well, judging from your slight accent and the fact that you were muttering something incomprehensible when you were lying on top of me, I assume that Italian is your first language. Which must mean that you live over there usually. So what are you doing in London?'

'Having a change from Italy.' His answer was so smooth and glib that she looked at him closely, wondering if he was hiding something. He caught her look and smiled. 'Plenty of doctors from EC countries come and work in England. It isn't unusual.'

'So where were you working last?'

'In a private clinic outside Milan.' He gave a rueful smile. 'Most of my patients were nothing like Kelly, I'm afraid.'

'Too posh to push?'

He smiled in appreciation. 'Something like that.'

'Well, it was decent of you to take a look at Kelly for me.' She glanced at him. 'Don't think I don't know that most doctors would have refused. Too worried about litigation.'

Carlo looked unconcerned. 'I'm well insured.'

And very experienced and self-confident. She also suspected that he would never refuse to help a patient. He was that type of man.

'This is where I live.' Zan stopped outside a block of flats and Carlo leaned against the wall, his eyes watchful.

'So...' he drawled softly. 'Are you going to invite me up?'

She stared at him, caught by the intensity of his gaze. Excitement curled in the pit of her stomach and she struggled to be sensible.

'I don't usually invite strangers up to my flat.'

His smile had a peculiar effect on her knees and she felt them wobble alarmingly. 'I'm very glad to hear that.' He moved fractionally closer to her, his eyes never leaving hers. 'But we've already kissed twice and spent an evening together so we're not exactly strangers.'

She laughed to disguise her awareness of him.

'We spent the evening in a filthy flat with a man who wanted to hit both of us. Is that your idea of a perfect first date?'

'It was different,' he admitted, his gaze dropping to her mouth and lingering there. 'You can trust me, Zan.'

She hesitated, common sense wrestling with temptation.

'I don't know anything about you.'

Except that he was strong, clever and stunningly good-looking.

'What do you want to know?' He smiled down at her. 'I'm Italian, I'm an obstetrician, I have one older brother and one younger sister. I also have a black eye.'

She smiled back and then looked at him cautiously. 'You're not married?'

His gaze didn't shift from hers. 'No wife. No kids.'

She bit her lip. Would it be such a big mistake to invite him up?

She paused a moment longer and then made up her mind. She pushed open the swing doors and led him into the deserted entrance hall. 'I'm on the top floor.'

They walked towards the lift and she pressed the button, watching the lift doors close and wondering what on earth she was doing, taking a total stranger back to her flat.

Was she mad?

Her brothers would have thrown a fit.

But then she'd spent most of the past twenty-four years being cautious, and frankly she was getting impatient with herself. It was time she lived a little. Time she trusted her own instincts.

And her instincts about Carlo were all good.

She loved his wicked sense of humour, the way the corners of his eyes creased when he smiled, and she loved his easy confidence. There was something about him that was tough and kind and, no matter how much she tried to pretend otherwise, the fact that he'd stepped in and rescued her made her insides squishy. It might not be politically correct to have a tough man looking after you but the truth was it had felt good.

Better than good.

It would be a long time before she forgot the feel of that hard muscle pressing her down onto the snowy pavement or the taste of his warm lips as he'd kissed her.

She shivered slightly with nerves and excitement as she remembered that kiss. Until tonight she'd always thought that kissing was a very overrated pastime.

She'd obviously been kissing the wrong men.

She sneaked a sideways look at him, still finding it hard to believe that he was a doctor. All the doctors she'd ever met were mild-mannered and academic or just plain arrogant. Carlo was none of those things. He was all muscle and strength, mixed with a wickedly sexy sense of humour.

He intercepted her look and gave her a smile that reminded her of his kiss. Hot and exciting.

She dragged some air into her lungs and leaned against the wall of the lift for support. If all Italian men looked like him she was moving to Italy.

The lift pinged as it arrived at her floor and she made an effort to stand upright.

'You'd better prepare yourself,' she warned him as she scrabbled in her pocket for the key. 'I call it the penthouse because it's on the top floor and the view are great, but trust me when I say that the resemblance ends there. When I win the Lottery I'm buying something bigger. You can't swing a cat in here...'

She pushed the key in the lock and then paused, aware that he was staring at her oddly. 'What? What have I said?'

'Why would you want to *swing* a cat?' His accent was marked as he repeated her words. 'I thought you English were supposed to like animals?'

'We do. Well, some of us do.' Zan grinned. 'It's just an expression.'

His eyes gleamed. 'Totally incomprehensible language. I thought my English was good, but evidently I still have a lot to learn.'

Carlo had gorgeous eyes—very dark brown and fringed with sinfully thick, dark lashes that he used to hide his expression when it suited him. And it suited him often. She suspected that he wasn't an easy man to read.

'Don't worry—I'll teach you.' Zan opened the door and walked into her flat, flicking on the light.

The pale wooden floor was covered in plastic packets and bags from various shops, and she shot him an embarrassed look as she started to scoop them all up.

'You needn't hide the packaging from me,' he said, his

tone amused. 'I was well aware that all that baby stuff you gave her was brand-new.'

She clutched the evidence to her chest and looked at him in dismay. 'Oh, no! I tried to rumple them and make them look old. Do you think they guessed?'

'I think Kelly was too pleased to notice.' He moved closer to her and removed one of the plastic wrappers from her grasp, lifting an eyebrow as he saw the price. 'Do you always spend your money on your patients?'

She blushed and snatched the wrapper back. 'No. Well, sometimes. I like Kelly and I feel sorry for her.'

He looked at her for a long moment and she felt the breath jam in her throat. Just looking at him made her legs shaky.

As if he'd guessed her thoughts, he gave a lopsided smile and strolled over to the huge windows that made up one wall of her tiny flat.

'Fantastic view.'

'Thanks.' She tugged the hat off her head and shook her dark hair like a kitten in a rainstorm. *Typical. She had a man to die for in her flat and she looked as though she'd been dunked in a puddle.* 'I've never bothered with curtains. No one can see in so it didn't seem worth it.'

'It's a nice flat.'

She smiled. 'Well, like I said, it's the penthouse, but when I win the Lottery I'm buying a bigger version.'

For a moment he didn't respond, and then he turned, a strange light in his eyes. 'You do the Lottery? Is money important to you?'

'No.' She tossed the rubbish into the bin and smiled cheerfully. 'Just what it buys. I love to dream, don't you?'

He sucked in a breath and looked taken aback. 'Well, I...'

'Oh, come on!' She tugged off her boots and coat and dropped onto the sofa, cross-legged. 'Everyone dreams of winning the Lottery. Even people who never remember to do it!'

He was looking at her curiously, arms folded across his broad chest. 'So what would you buy?'

'I don't know, the usual things...' She shrugged. 'A house in a better area, a car so that I don't have to walk around at night.'

'Would you give up your job?'

'Oh, no!' Her expression was horrified. 'I love my job. And just think, if I won money I'd be able to rehouse Kelly and Mike without having to bow and scrape to Social Services all the time.'

Carlo turned back to the window. 'You'd have a job to beat this view.'

'Nice, isn't it? They've converted so much of the Docklands area into housing and it's a pretty good place to live.' She glanced round her with satisfaction. She liked her flat. It was small, but it was cosy and homely and all hers. 'Make the most of it. It's pretty small now, but after tomorrow it's going to get even smaller.'

'What's happening tomorrow?' He moved away from the window and strolled towards her.

'I'm buying my Christmas tree,' she said proudly, 'and it's going to be *big*.'

'Ah.' He folded his arms across his chest and his sexy dark eyes twinkled at her. 'So size matters to you?'

'In Christmas trees, definitely.' Zan was laughing at the innuendo and trying to control the frantic fluttering in her stomach. 'I love everything about Christmas. I used to buy my tree on the first day of December, but the needles always fell off by Christmas Day and I got fed up with staring at decorated twigs so now I make myself wait. It's an exercise in self-discipline. What about you? Do you like Christmas?'

He hesitated and then nodded. 'I suppose so.'

'But you're sad because you won't be at home this year?' She tilted her head on one side and looked at him. 'I know the feeling. I'm working this Christmas so I won't be able to get home until New Year. But I've written my letter to Santa and he knows I'm here so all my presents should still arrive.'

He leaned broad shoulders against the wall and watched her, and she was breathlessly aware of how big he seemed in her tiny flat.

Big and male.

'You've written to Santa?'

'Of course! I've sent him my list. How else will he know what I want?' She ticked them off on her fingers. 'Diamond earrings, cashmere jumper, silky underwear—you know the sort of thing.'

'Diamond earrings?' His gaze slid down to her torn jeans. 'You don't strike me as a diamond earrings sort of girl.'

'Don't judge by appearances. I've never been given the chance,' she told him gloomily. 'With four brothers my childhood was all rugby boots and Action Man. Every single Christmas I'd get the same stuff as them. Don't get me wrong. My parents are great and I love them. But somewhere along the line they forgot I was a girl. I would have given anything for something pink and girly.'

He blinked. 'Pink and girly?'

'You know, something feminine. What about you? What do you want for Christmas?'

There was a long silence, and when he finally spoke his gaze was disturbingly direct. 'You.' He spoke the word softly and then paused, his dark eyes holding hers. 'I want you, Zan.'

There was a hot, pulsing silence and she stared at him, her heart in her mouth and her palms damp.

His words shocked and excited her and for a moment

she had no idea how to respond. The truth was she wanted him too, but the feeling scared her.

She'd only known him for one evening.

'I don't do one-night stands.'

'Good.' His dark eyes didn't shift from hers. 'I'm not interested in just one night.'

She looked into those stunning dark eyes and felt her insides tumble. Suddenly overwhelmed by his directness and the intensity of her own feelings, she jumped to her feet and looked at him nervously.

He was so different from the men she normally mixed with. They seemed younger somehow. More boyish. But there was nothing boyish about Carlo. He was all man. A man who knew exactly what he wanted and went straight for it.

And she couldn't forget the way he kissed.

'Where did you come from?' She wrapped her arms around her middle defensively. 'I mean, one minute my life is thoroughly predictable and full of men who bore me to tears and then the next...'

He lifted a dark eyebrow and prompted her gently, his Italian accent suddenly pronounced, 'The next?'

Her heart was hammering in her chest. She didn't know which was sexier, the tone of his voice or the look in his eyes. 'The next I find myself lying on the pavement, kissing a total stranger.'

'Is that a complaint?' His dark eyes teased her and her breath came in little pants.

'Not exactly. I'm just not used to kissing in the street in front of an audience.'

'But now we have no audience.' He gave a smile that sent her pulse racing and she lost her nerve and took a step backwards.

'Do you want coffee?'

'No.' He moved towards her, standing so close she could feel the warmth from his body against hers.

Zan's heart was pounding frantically. Just remembering what his kiss had felt like was enough to make her knees start to tremble. He was breathtakingly attractive.

But she shouldn't be kissing men she didn't know.

Her eyes dropped to his mouth and her lips parted in breathless anticipation.

Or maybe she should.

Still unsure, she gave him a nervous smile. 'I still haven't put ice on your eye.'

'Right now it isn't my eye that needs the ice.' He pulled her against him and lowered his head, their breath mingling as his mouth hovered above hers.

She shivered with expectation, waiting for him to kiss her, the excitement and anticipation stealing every breath from her body. His lips brushed hers, teasing her lightly, and he gave her a wicked smile, fully aware of the tension he was creating between them.

And then finally he kissed her properly.

And this time the kiss was different.

What they'd shared on the pavement had been exploratory and fun, but this—this was a purposeful seduction, and Zan realised immediately that if this was how kissing could feel then she'd never been kissed before.

Carlo kissed as though he'd invented excitement. The touch of his mouth was a wholly sexual experience that swamped her inexperienced body with unfamiliar sensations of such intensity that she squirmed against him in a purely female plea for satisfaction.

His mouth still on hers, he lifted her arms and wrapped them around his neck and then pulled her hard against him, his tongue delving into her mouth with devastating thoroughness, encouraging her more hesitant response.

It was the most intimate experience of her life. The

skilled sweep of his tongue, the hard ridge of his erection pressed against her and the pounding of her heart against her breastbone.

She breathed in his scent, felt the roughness of his jaw against her, tasted his maleness and felt overwhelmed by a fevered desperation that defied logic.

His touch was totally addictive and when he finally dragged his mouth away from hers she sucked in some air, so shaken by her own reaction that she couldn't bring herself to look him in the eye.

She'd never been kissed by anyone as skilled as him before.

He slid his strong fingers through her hair and tilted her head so that she was forced to look at him.

His dark eyes shimmered with raw hunger, but he veiled it quickly and gave a lopsided smile.

'I don't think we'd better do that for too long, *cara mia*,' he said dryly. 'We might both explode.'

Totally blown away by his kiss, Zan tried to speak and failed.

He touched her cheek with a gentle finger. 'You know what?' He was totally relaxed and easy with himself. 'I could really do with taking a shower. My jeans are soaked because someone threw me on my back in a puddle.'

She loved the way he took the seriousness out of every situation. 'You're joking! Who would do an evil thing like that?'

'I can't imagine, but when I track them down they're going to be punished.' He pulled her against him and gave her another lingering kiss. 'Maybe we should get out of these wet clothes before we both freeze. Can I put my jeans in your tumble-drier and take a shower?'

She nodded and gestured towards the kitchen. 'It's through there. Help yourself.'

His eyes were very dark. 'Are you going to join me?'

No.

Resolving to be more daring was all very well, but you couldn't change the habit of a lifetime in an hour!

It was all too fast.

Zan shook her head and he gave her a warm smile and strolled into her kitchen, emerging moments later with an apologetic look on his face and his jeans dangling from one hand.

'I don't know how to use a tumble-drier.'

Carlo's humble confession broke the ice and she laughed, trying not to look at his tanned, strong legs. He had an incredible physique—athletic and powerful.

No wonder the muggers had run.

'More of the macho Italian guy stuff, I suppose? Who does your washing at home? Or maybe I shouldn't ask that question.'

'I have a housekeeper,' he told her, and she walked over to him and took the wet jeans out of his hand, still keeping her eyes averted.

'Well, she hasn't trained you very well.' She popped them into the tumble-drier, turned the dial and started the machine. 'I assume you know how the shower works, or does your housekeeper do that bit, too?'

His midnight-dark eyes gleamed wickedly. 'I'm OK with the shower, but I've never really got the hang of undressing myself.'

No man should be allowed to have a smile that sexy. It had a lethal effect on her pulse-rate.

'Well, if you don't want another black eye you'd better learn quickly,' she said, ignoring his laughter and hurrying past him. 'I'll fetch you a towel.'

The shower was running by the time she returned with the towel and she half opened the door and talked through the crack.

'I'll leave the towel on the floor.'

'Pardon?' His voice was muffled from the water and she leaned in slightly further, averting her eyes from the shower cubicle.

'I said I'll leave the towel on the floor.'

'I can't hear you.'

She sidled in a bit further and strong arms grabbed her and hauled her under the steaming jet of water.

'You pig!' Laughing and squealing, she thumped him hard, spluttering and screwing up her eyes against the water. 'What are you *doing*?'

'Economising on water.' He was laughing, too, and she gasped as he pulled her close and kissed her, ignoring the water that was raining down on both of them.

She leaned into him and kissed him back, and suddenly the laughter stopped and the kissing intensified until their mouths fused hungrily, the chemistry a living, powerful force between them.

Her whole body was singing with excitement and suddenly she was breathlessly aware of his arousal and the fact that he was totally naked.

An unbearable ache was building between her thighs, but when she felt his fingers on the zip of her soaked jeans she reached down and grabbed his hands, stopping him.

What was she doing?

His skill and experience had her at flashpoint in seconds, but the speed with which he could reduce her to a shivering mass of desperation made her nervous. She'd only ever kissed boys before and Carlo certainly wasn't that. He was a fully adult male and he wasn't playing games.

'Wait—it's too fast...' The water was streaming over her hair and down her back and he reached out a hand to stem the flow, speaking softly to her in Italian as he held her against him.

'You want me to stop?' He switched to English and she struggled to control her response.

'Yes— No…' She was shaking against him and he gave a groan and slid a warm hand over her back.

'Have you any idea how much I want you?'

Zan gave him a shaky smile, breathlessly aware of his masculinity. *He had a fantastic body*. His confidence with his own sexuality was in complete contrast to her own inexperience and she felt completely out of her depth.

From the moment she'd stared into his eyes in the snowy street she'd decided that even if she only had sex once in her whole life, she wanted it to be with this man. But now that the moment had come she felt hideously unsure.

Carlo probably thought that any woman who was prepared to kiss him in a public place was equally experienced and relaxed about sex.

She was still panicking when she felt a warm, soft towel draped around her shoulders.

'Take off your wet jeans and go and put on your least provocative outfit,' Carlo said, his voice infinitely gentle as he stepped back and let her step out of the shower.

She bit her lip and looked at him anxiously. 'I…thought we were going to…'

'Well, we're not,' he said softly. 'At least, not yet. You're not totally sure and I *want* you to be totally sure.'

She hesitated and shook her head, painfully self-conscious. 'It's just a bit fast. I don't know you— I can't—'

'So we slow it down.'

He made it sound perfectly simple and she looked at him shyly, surprised that he wasn't more annoyed with her. 'And you're OK with that?'

'Well, I'll need a lot of cold showers,' he admitted ruefully, 'but we've already agreed that if I step out of line you can black my other eye, so I'll do my best to hold back as long as I can. Now, go and get dressed quickly.'

When Zan arrived back in the sitting room Carlo had the towel wrapped around his hips, his black hair damp and tousled from the shower as he flicked through her CD collection.

'Carlo.' She came to a halt in front of him, her smile hesitant. 'Are you angry?'

He glanced up. 'Of course not.' He seemed surprised by the question. 'Why would I be?'

Zan thought of all the conversations she'd overheard when her brothers hadn't known she was listening, and bit her lip.

'Because I made you think that I... I'm sorry if you thought I... I didn't mean to lead you on...'

Ebony brows came together in a frown. 'You are always entitled to say no, *cara mia*.'

'But I didn't want to say no,' she said quickly, a blush touching her cheek. 'Not exactly. But it all seemed a bit quick and— I know you're very confident, but, you see, I've never actually done it before.'

She broke off, painfully aware of the stunned expression in his gorgeous eyes.

She should never have told him.

The silence seemed to stretch for ever, and when he finally spoke his voice was rough.

'Then I'm doubly pleased that your first time wasn't in a shower, *tesoro*. We can do a great deal better than that when the time comes.'

She looked at him, her heart missing a beat as the warmth in his eyes and the full implication of his words hit her.

'You still want to?'

'What do you think?' Carlo moved towards her and cupped her face in his hands. 'I'm sorry if I moved too fast. It never occurred to me that—'

'I didn't want to tell you. I thought it might put you off,' she muttered, and he laughed.

'In that case, you have a great deal to learn about Italian men, *cara mia*.' He looked into her face, smug male satisfaction reflected in his dark eyes. 'We are a hideously jealous, possessive race. We are not good at sharing. We like a woman to be ours and ours alone.'

His alone.

The thought sent heat flaring through Zan and she pulled away from him. 'I'll see if your trousers are dry.'

He followed her to the kitchen, leaning broad shoulders against the doorway as he watched her.

'I cannot believe that you're still a virgin,' he observed, lush dark lashes shielding his gorgeous eyes. 'Your brothers obviously did a good job at protecting you.'

She reached into the tumble-drier and dragged out his trousers. 'Every time a boy became remotely interested in me they worked really hard to scare him off. Amazing teamwork and family unity. They succeeded every time.'

He lifted an eyebrow. 'And the men in question were willing to be scared off?'

She handed him the trousers and their fingers brushed together. 'I suppose they were boys, really, and my brothers must have been pretty daunting.'

'And what about now you're grown-up?'

'Now they just rely on my natural wariness to keep me out of mischief.' She looked at him anxiously, suddenly aware that she'd only known him for a few hours. How had she ever let him so close to her so quickly?

'It's OK, Zan.' His voice was incredibly gentle. 'I don't go off with women I've just met either. We'll take this slowly and see where it ends up.'

The thought of where it might end up sent her stomach dropping to the floor.

'Do you want some coffee?'

Maybe caffeine would clear her mind.

'What sort of coffee?' His gorgeous eyes narrowed and he looked at her suspiciously. 'At home we clean floors with what you English call coffee.'

She stuck her chin in the air and gave him a superior look. 'I'll have you know I make the best cappuccino in London—'

'Well, that isn't saying much— Ouch!' He winced as she thumped him and his eyes creased with humour. 'In that case, I'll put my jeans on while you make it.'

She made two steaming mugs of cappuccino, tipped some home-made shortbread onto a plate and walked back into the living room.

Carlo sprawled on the cushions by the floor-to-ceiling window, staring down at the Thames.

There was something peaceful and Christmassy about the lights sparkling along the bank, and he relished the fact that for a rare moment in time no one actually knew where he was.

There was going to be hell to pay later.

'I always love London at night.' Zan knelt down next to him and handed him the coffee. 'It's magical, isn't it? And you can't see the grime.'

'All cities are grimy in the day. You should see Milan— smoggy and noisy.' Carlo took a sip of coffee and looked at her in surprise. 'Mmm. You're right, you do make good coffee. This is excellent.'

He'd given up trying to find a decent cup of coffee in England, but she'd managed to produce one.

Maybe it was an omen.

She'd changed into another pair of jeans and a soft cream jumper that just seemed to make her more huggable. She was soft and womanly and so *alive* that everything about her made him smile.

And her shy confession had affected him deeply.

He'd never been with anyone as inexperienced as her before.

'Come here.' He put his coffee down and reached for her, trying to keep his tone neutral and unthreatening. Inside he was a raging mass of male hormones but he had no intention of letting her see that.

He was already feeling guilty that he'd pushed her too far in the shower.

Without the slightest hesitation she snuggled into his arms and they lay together on the cushions, staring out of the window.

She was so trusting.

Carlo felt an uncomfortable twist of guilt at the knowledge that he was deceiving her. On the other hand he couldn't deny that he was enjoying the fact that she didn't know who he was.

She lifted her head and looked at him, a touch of shyness in her twinkling eyes.

'You like my coffee?'

He liked everything about her.

Unable to resist her, he gave a groan and rolled her back onto the cushions, shifting so that he was lying on top of her. Careful to keep his weight off her, he lowered his head and took her mouth, exploring its sweetness, trying to keep the kiss light and teasing.

He failed.

Zan's response to his kiss was so hot and eager that desire ripped through him and he took the kiss a stage further. With every skilled stroke of his tongue he felt her trembling increase and the hand resting on her ribcage felt the rapid pounding of her heart.

The knowledge that she wanted him as badly as he wanted her did nothing for his self-control and he slid his hand under the hem of her jumper and felt her skin, warm and soft under the tips of his fingers. She gasped against his mouth as his fingers found her nipples and he felt his erection throb within the confines of his jeans.

Next time he met up with Zan, he *definitely* wouldn't be wearing jeans.

Aware that he was testing his self-control to its limits, he dragged his mouth away from hers, moved his hand and sucked in some air.

If kissing her drove him this wild then what was going to happen when he finally made love to her?

Out of breath, and shaken by the whole experience of kissing Zan, he rolled onto his back, taking her with him, trying to make sense of the way he felt.

She burrowed into his chest and then finally she lifted her head and looked at him, shyness and question mingling in her green eyes.

'Why did you stop?'

Was she really that innocent?

Carlo gave a wry smile. 'Why do you think?'

Her eyes widened and her cheeks flushed pink. 'You wanted me?'

'You could say that.'

But it would have been an understatement.

'You're an amazing kisser.'

He was tempted to suggest that she sample the rest of his skills, but he didn't want to hear her say no a second time that night.

'You're incredibly good to kiss.'

'Do you know that you talk in Italian when you kiss? You sort of murmur against my mouth and it's so sexy.'

She was all tousled and warm from his kiss and he wondered if his erection was ever going to subside.

'It's my first language,' he reminded her, grateful that she didn't speak it. He'd said some things that would have probably have made her run a mile.

'I love your accent,' she said dreamily, putting her chin

on her palm and staring at him with those huge green eyes. 'Say something to me in Italian now. Go on—anything.'

He kept his face serious. 'Cappuccino.'

'Oh, very funny.' She rested a hand on his chest and he reached for her and pulled her on top of him.

'*Io voglio te,*' he said softly, and she looked at him curiously.

'What does that mean?'

I want you.

But he shouldn't be telling her that. He wasn't in a position to offer her anything except trouble and hurt.

Suddenly feeling hideously guilty for taking advantage of her, Carlo pulled her close, his voice gruff as he spoke. 'It means you're a pretty sexy chick.'

'Does it?' She chuckled and leaned forward to kiss him. 'I'm obviously going to have to learn Italian. Will you teach me?'

'I can think of other things I'd rather teach you.' He smiled at her, thinking that she was the most gorgeous woman he'd ever seen.

Flushed and sparkly-eyed and full of humour and warmth.

He never, ever wanted to give her up.

He frowned at his own thoughts. Of course he'd want to give her up eventually. Commitment was the very last thing on his agenda. Circumstances meant that he'd ceased to trust women long ago and he was incredibly wary of relationships.

But this was different because she didn't know who he was.

'You look serious all of a sudden.' Zan looked up at him, her eyes concerned.

He forced a smile. 'I was just thinking that I start a new job in six hours.'

And his security people would be out there combing the streets for him.

She gasped and glanced at the clock. 'I'd forgotten about work. You'd better go!'

He bent his head and kissed her gently. 'Maybe I don't want to go.'

'Well, you can't turn up at the hospital wearing my clothes,' she teased, her eyes slightly shy as she looked at him. 'Even if you don't sleep, surely you need to go home and get changed. Where is home, by the way?'

He hesitated and then rolled away from her. 'I'm staying somewhere temporary at the moment—nowhere special.'

His brother's three-million-pound penthouse apartment overlooking Hyde Park.

'Right.' She gave him a sympathetic look. 'Well, that's not very nice over Christmas. You need a home, not somewhere temporary.'

He pulled his jumper over his head and stared at her. 'What are you suggesting?'

She gave a nervous shrug. 'You could stay here.' The minute the words had left her mouth she wrapped her arms around herself and bit her lip. 'Forget I said that.'

'What if I don't want to forget it?'

She covered her face with her hands and shook her head. 'I don't know myself when I'm with you. I'm doing really strange things. Like inviting you up to my flat when you're a total stranger and inviting you for Christmas. I've gone crazy.'

He couldn't think of a better way to spend Christmas than moving in with Zan and being surrounded by her warmth and laughter and her incredible body.

But he couldn't do it.

His life was just too complicated at the moment. Complicated and dangerous and he wouldn't put her at risk.

And he could see that she was really confused about the strength of her own feelings.

Carlo stepped forward and gently pulled her hands away from her face. 'As you said earlier, we probably need to slow the pace a little. Let's see how it goes, shall we?'

She hesitated, and then gave a smile that was just a little too bright. 'Good idea.'

He sighed and covered her soft lips with a finger. 'I know what you're thinking and you're wrong. You're thinking that when I walk out of this door that's going to be it.'

Colour touched her cheekbones. 'I've got four brothers,' she muttered. 'I know all the lines they use.'

Zan was incredibly brave and dignified, but he had enough experience with women to know that she was as attracted to him as he was to her.

'I'm not using any of those lines,' Carlo said firmly, ignoring the flash of guilt that exploded inside him.

He *was* deceiving her.

And he probably ought to walk away from her and never see her again because he wasn't in a position to give this woman anything but grief.

But he wasn't going to do that.

He had to see her again.

'Where the hell have you been?'

Carlo glanced at Matteo Parini, his long-time friend and his father's chief of security. 'I went for a walk.'

He shrugged his shoulders out of his coat.

'For five hours?'

'Calm down, Matt, or you'll have a stroke,' Carlo said mildly. 'I left a message on your mobile.'

'Five hours ago!!'

'So?' Carlo gave a shrug. 'I met a girl.'

A girl who had no idea who he was.

For possibly the first time in his life Carlo was sure that a woman was interested in him for himself alone, and he found the knowledge oddly satisfying. Zan didn't know anything about his money.

There was an ominous silence and Matt stiffened with disbelief. '*A girl?* You've been in London for one evening and already you've met someone? That's fast, even for you.'

Not just someone.

The one.

Carlo frowned at his own thoughts. Women had been trying to trap him into a serious relationship for years but he'd never been remotely tempted.

Until tonight.

'Do you believe in love at first sight?'

Matt stared at him with naked incredulity. 'I can't believe you just asked me that.'

Carlo grinned. He couldn't believe it either. 'Well?'

'Only when I've had several drinks,' Matt responded wryly, shaking his head as he scrutinised Carlo's face. 'Tell me you're not serious. You've only just met her.'

'I know that.'

But she'd affected him in a way that no other woman had before.

Matt let out a long breath and tried to reason with him. 'You can't do this. Not now. You're supposed to be keeping a low profile. What if she goes to the press? The whole idea of the false name was to fool the press.'

'She won't go to the press,' Carlo said easily. 'She doesn't know who I am.'

'Yet.' Matt lifted an eyebrow meaningfully but Carlo refused to lose his cool.

'Relax. This isn't Italy. And I don't think she's the type to read glitzy magazines.'

Matt sighed. 'Well, at least take me with you next time.'

It was Carlo's turn to lift an eyebrow. 'I never thought you were kinky.'

'I'll wait outside,' Matt growled, and Carlo gave a grudging smile.

'You're a good friend, but I don't need a watchdog.'

'Really?' Matt looked at his cheek. 'So how did you get that?'

Carlo lifted a hand and touched the bruise with the tips of his fingers, a soft smile touching his mouth. 'I was attacked.'

'Attacked?' Matt stared at him in growing dismay and Carlo's grin widened.

'By the woman. I tried to rescue her—'

'And she hit you?' Matt looked stunned and Carlo started to laugh.

'We had a misunderstanding. She didn't realise I was rescuing her.'

Matt laughed too. 'No wonder you think you're in love with her. There's something very sexy about a confident woman.'

Carlo gave a half-smile, knowing that only part of Zan was confident and feisty. The other part was feminine and shy, and the combination was mind-blowing.

Matt's smile faded. 'Look, you feel this way because she doesn't know who you are. It's just the novelty.'

Carlo thought about it. 'It isn't that.'

Matt shot him a frustrated look. 'This is a really, really bad time for you to get involved with someone, Carlo. You don't know anything about her.'

Carlo's expression darkened. 'And she doesn't know anything about me. There is no way she'd be involved in all this, if that's what you're suggesting. She's totally innocent.'

Completely innocent.

The thought made his insides tighten and he gave a smile of pure male possession.

He was going to make her his.

All his.

Matt wasn't so easily distracted. 'Let's be honest about this for a moment. You left Italy to draw those lunatics away from your family—to tempt them into following you. I still think it was a bad idea, especially as you're so careless about security.'

'Careless?' Carlo's eyes gleamed. 'Oh, believe me, I'm not careless.'

He was totally alert and more than ready to face the threat.

'Well, even if she doesn't shop you to the press, associating with this girl could put *her* at risk. They could use her to get to you,' Matt growled, obviously totally frustrated by Carlo's lack of co-operation. 'Don't think the false name is going to fool them. We did that to lose the press as much as anything. The men behind the threats are pros. I'm willing to bet they already know who you are and where you are.'

Carlo's smiled. 'Of course they do.'

He was under no illusions about his current position.

Matt frowned. 'You can't see her again. At least, not until this mess is sorted out.'

'I know that, too.' Carlo's smile faded and he rubbed long fingers over his forehead.

Everything Matt said was true. He had left Italy to draw the men who were threatening him away from his family.

To see Zan again could be risky for her. But he knew he couldn't give her up.

Maybe he could stall her and hope that the guys who were threatening him came out into the open quickly.

On the other hand, if he was honest, he was enjoying

living his life as someone else for the time being. He liked the fact that Zan didn't know about his true circumstances.

For the first time in his life he was able to have a normal relationship with a woman without his money getting in the way. There was no way he was letting that go.

'There's another thing to consider.' Matt's tone was cautious. 'Even if she doesn't know who you are now, it's bound to come out soon. And she'll be hurt that you didn't tell her. And a hurt woman—'

'Is dangerous,' Carlo finished flatly, pacing across the apartment and staring down at the snow-covered trees.

'She could go to the papers.'

Carlo frowned, knowing that it was true. His family had been hurt on numerous occasions when girls he and his brother had dated had later sold their stories to the newspapers. It was one of the reasons he was extremely careful in his relationships with the opposite sex.

He couldn't believe that Zan would do a thing like that.

But he'd been burned before. Badly.

He stirred and looked at his friend. 'She isn't the type. She's special.'

'Special enough to forgive you when she discovers that you've lied?'

Carlo let out a long breath. 'I certainly hope so.'

If she wasn't, then his life had just become even more complicated.

CHAPTER THREE

'ALL right, what's going on?' Kim, Zan's best friend and the sister in charge of the antenatal clinic, glanced up curiously as they prepared for the morning clinic. 'I've just told you we've got a full clinic, a locum doctor who doesn't know the ropes and two off sick. Why are you grinning? Did I miss the joke?'

Zan picked up a stack of notes and hugged them to her chest. Her insides were so churned up with excitement that she hadn't even managed breakfast. All she could think about was Carlo.

'I'm just happy.'

'That's what worries me,' Kim said dryly. 'Why would you be happy, given that by the end of the day you'll have blisters on both feet and a headache bigger than Africa?'

'I don't care about blisters. I met someone.' She tried to sound nonchalant and then wondered why she was even bothering. Kim was her best friend and they told each other everything.

'You met someone? *When?* We worked together yesterday and your smile was normal-sized then.' Kim looked at her, stunned, and Zan laughed.

'I met him last night.'

'Last night? So it wasn't quick or anything?' Kim shook her head in disbelief. 'Zan, I hate to be the one to point this out, but falling for men in one night isn't your style. In fact, correct me if I'm wrong, but you've never fallen for anyone, no matter how many nights were involved. You invented the word "cautious". I'm the reckless one in this friendship.'

Zan shrugged. 'So maybe it's time I changed.'

Kim glanced around to check that no one was within earshot and lowered her voice. 'So did you...*you know*?'

'Kim!' Zan pretended to look shocked and then grinned. 'No. We didn't. But I've made up my mind I'm going to. He's going to be my Christmas present to myself. I'm fed up with being cautious and he's gorgeous.'

'Obviously.' Kim sounded faint. 'He's managed to achieve in one night what the whole male race has been struggling with for years. I can't wait to meet him.'

Zan dipped her head, deciding not to mention that the locum and her new man were one and the same. Her relationship was too new to expose it to one of Kim's indiscreet comments.

'Anyway, if you could pull yourself down off the cloud you're sitting on, we need to get this clinic started,' Kim said brightly. 'And when we've finished that, we've got a tree to decorate.'

'That's OK.' Zan smiled. She loved decorating Christmas trees and she wasn't afraid of hard work. 'So where do you want me to start?'

'Here in clinic, keeping an eye on my locum, who's in Room 1,' Kim told her, and Zan fought to control her expression. If the new locum was the person she thought he was then she intended to keep much more than an eye on him.

Her heart banging against her ribcage and her hands suddenly shaking, she picked up a pile of notes and walked towards her room.

It connected with the room next door, and through the open door she could see Carlo sitting at the desk, stethoscope looped around his neck, reading through a set of notes.

It was the first time she'd seen him in daylight and her heart missed a beat.

Her first thought was that he was stunningly good-looking. Dressed in a dark suit, he had an air of strength and authority that made her catch her breath.

Her second thought was that he didn't look English.

Her eyes slid over his short, cropped hair, rested for a moment on his olive skin and dark jaw and then dropped down to those powerful shoulders.

He looked completely and thoroughly Italian.

She knew she was staring but she couldn't help herself, and when he glanced up and saw her standing there his face broke into a smile that made her remember why she'd ended up semi-naked in the shower with him after only a few hours' acquaintance.

He was the sexiest man she'd ever met.

He rose to his feet in a fluid movement and strolled across to her, his gaze heating as he looked at her.

'*Buongiorno*—good morning.'

'Good morning.' Suddenly she felt ridiculously shy and lifted a hand to smooth her dark hair behind her ear.

He gave a low groan and glanced over his shoulder to make sure that no one was listening. 'Don't do that or I'll never get any work done this morning.'

Before she could answer, Kim walked into the room, clutching a pile of notes.

'Mr Bennett?'

At first Carlo didn't react, but he must have seen something in Zan's eyes because he suddenly shook himself and turned to the other woman.

'Yes. Sorry, sister.' He cleared his throat. 'I was miles away.'

Zan frowned, puzzled. It was as if he hadn't heard his own name. Was she really that distracting?

Kim beamed at him. 'I just came to say that you're very welcome, and if there's anything at all you need while you're working here, you can ask one of us. We're very informal here. Do call me Kim. And this is Suzannah Wilde, but we call her Zan. She'll be working in the room next door so that you can see patients together when the need arises.'

'Well, that's good to know.' Carlo's eyes gleamed slightly and Zan turned away so that Kim wouldn't see her blushing.

Kim was chattering away to both of them, oblivious to the tension between the two of them. 'We've got Mrs Hughes in the waiting room; she's expecting twins. We try not to keep her waiting too long for obvious reasons.' Kim handed Carlo the notes. 'Have you had much experience with multiple pregnancies, Mr Bennett?'

'Call me Carlo, and the answer to your question is, yes, plenty.' Carlo stretched out a lean brown hand and took the notes from her. 'One of my special interests is infertility, and I'm afraid one of the consequences of infertility treatment is an increase in multiple pregnancies, even though we do try to avoid that happening. I delivered several sets of twins and two sets of triplets last year.'

'Mrs Hughes is thirty-seven weeks pregnant and has two more children at home, both under five,' Zan told him, trying to keep her tone professional. 'It's pretty hard for her to get enough rest. Her blood pressure was borderline last time.'

Carlo nodded and flicked his eyes over the notes. 'Let's get her in. Do Zan and I see her together or separately?'

'Together. Zan is her midwife,' Kim said immediately. 'Has she explained how we work here?'

Carlo shook his head and looked at Zan expectantly.

'We try and give continuity of care whenever we can,' Zan explained, 'so, instead of working in one place, we all rotate. One day I might be in clinic and the next I might be on the labour ward. Basically we try and follow the patient, at least up until they have their baby. After that I'm afraid they get whoever is on the ward.'

Carlo listened carefully. 'So you see them in clinic and you deliver them?'

'That's the idea. We divide the midwives into teams, so the woman should at least be familiar with someone from the team. It means that they don't go into labour and find themselves being delivered by someone they've never met before,' Zan explained, and then gave a gasp and turned to Kim. 'I forgot to tell you—I saw Kelly Turner last night.'

Kim sighed. 'I hardly dare ask. And?'

'Well, she wasn't great,' Zan confessed, deciding not to mention that Carlo had been there, too. 'She's thirty-four weeks pregnant now, she looks tired and her uterus isn't the size it should be. I tried to get her to come in for a scan but Mike wasn't having it.'

'If we're not careful there's going to be a tragedy there,' Kim muttered. 'I'll have a word with the bosses and let them know what's going on and I'll speak to Social Services again. Any luck with the housing?'

'Not yet.' Zan's eyes twinkled. 'But I'm working on it.'

Kim grinned. 'They have my sympathies. What I want to know is how did you find time to see Kelly *and* meet a man?' She glanced at Carlo and winked. 'You'd better watch her concentration this morning. She met someone last night and now she's in love.'

Oh, thank you, Kim!

Zan closed her eyes and stifled a groan. Why, oh, why had she been so stupid as to tell her friend?

Carlo cleared his throat. 'Well, that's nice.'

Even without looking at him Zan could sense his amusement, and she backed towards the door.

'I'll go and tell Mrs Hughes she can come in, if you're ready.'

'Oh, I'll do that,' Kim said immediately. 'You and Carlo had better have a quick chat before you start seeing patients. By the way, what happened to your eye?'

Carlo lifted a hand to his cheek. 'Oh. I, er, had an accident.'

'Right.' Kim grinned and as soon as she'd left the room Carlo lifted his eyes to Zan's, the laughter in them unmistakable.

'A very interesting accident. So, who's this man you're in love with?'

'I never said I was in love,' she said hastily. 'Kim has a vivid imagination, that's all.'

'So you're *not* in love?'

She knew he was teasing her and her face flamed. 'I don't fall in love with men I've only just met.'

'Ouch. Is that a put-down?'

She looked at him and smiled shyly. 'I'm buying my tree tonight. If you'll lend me those muscles again, I'll cook you supper.'

His smile faded and there was no missing the sudden tension in his frame. 'Zan, about tonight…'

She saw the hesitation and felt the colour rush to her cheeks.

He'd had second thoughts.

Oh, damn, damn, damn. How could she have been so stupid?

A man as experienced as him certainly wouldn't want to be bothered with a virgin.

'Don't worry, I'm strong enough to carry the tree myself,' she said quickly, looking away and missing the frown that touched his brows. 'We'd better get going. This clinic sometimes runs until early afternoon if we dawdle. I'll call Mrs Hughes.' Without giving him a chance to speak, Zan left the room and sought sanctuary in the waiting area. She saw her patient immediately and managed to produce a smile.

'We're ready for you, Mrs Hughes.'

Carlo closed his eyes and cursed softly in Italian.

Zan thought he didn't want to see her again.

He was in an impossible situation. He'd promised Matt that he wouldn't see her again, at least for the time being, but that was going to hurt her badly and frankly *he* didn't feel too great about it either. But if he carried on then eventually he was going to have to confess that he'd been withholding significant information about himself, and additionally he could be putting her at risk.

Whichever route he took, he was going to hurt her.

She walked into the room at that moment, the twinkle missing from her gorgeous green eyes.

'This is Helen Hughes.' She smiled at the lady with her and helped her up onto the examination couch. 'You might as well see us both at the same time, Helen. It will save us asking the same questions.'

Carlo introduced himself and tried to drag his mind back to the job in hand. He gave the patient a warm smile and walked over to the couch. 'How are you feeling?'

'Pretty awful,' Helen Hughes confessed immediately. 'I've got terrible backache and indigestion which keeps me awake at night.'

Carlo nodded. 'Because you are carrying two babies, your uterus is that much larger than that of a mother who is pregnant with one child. I'm afraid that all the normal problems of pregnancy are often worse when you are expecting twins.'

Helen pulled a face and rubbed her back. 'Tell me about it. And it doesn't help that I already have two children to look after.' She exchanged a wry smile with Zan. 'We thought we'd have one more baby and look what happened.'

Carlo smiled. 'Is there a history of twins in your family?'

Helen nodded. 'I'm a twin and my aunt and my sister both had twins. I suppose I'm lucky I only had one set!'

Zan checked Helen's blood pressure and tested her urine sample for evidence of protein.

'That's all fine, Helen.' She showed the results to Carlo, who nodded.

'I'd like to feel your stomach, if that's all right.' He helped Helen wriggle down on the examining couch and then assessed the size of the uterus and the way the babies were lying.

Helen looked at him curiously. 'Can you tell which is which?'

'The first twin is lying head down in what we call a longitudinal position,' Carlo said immediately, and Helen's eyes widened.

'That's very impressive. The last doctor I had didn't have a clue! He had to scan me.'

'It can be hard when there are two babies,' Carlo admitted. 'Sometimes we need a scan to assess precisely how they are lying, but twins and triplets are a special interest of mine. Where I work in Italy, we also run an infertility clinic and, as you probably know, one of the consequences of infertility treatment is sometimes multiple births. We try to avoid it wherever we can, but I have more experience than most in delivering twins and triplets.'

'Oh.' Helen looked at him with a new respect. 'The doctor I saw here last time had never even delivered twins before. I have to confess it didn't fill me with confidence. Will you deliver me?'

Carlo smiled. 'That depends on when you have the babies. I will try to.'

'Well, I certainly hope you do, and that leads me to my next question,' Helen said promptly. 'When do you think they're coming? I'm going to need help with the other two and I daren't invite my mother too far in advance or my husband will leave home, especially at Christmas. I've already wrapped the children's presents and frozen enough food for an army.'

'So it's a wonder that your blood pressure isn't higher,' Carlo said dryly, finishing his examination and helping her to sit up. 'The answer to your question is that it is unusual for a twin pregnancy to last for the full forty weeks. Most women go into labour at about thirty-seven weeks, which is where you are now.'

Helen stared at him. 'So do you think it will be soon?'

Carlo smiled. 'In all probability, yes, but you might last until after Christmas.'

'I hope I do.' Helen looked worried. 'There's no way my husband could cope with two children under five, my mother *and* a raw turkey.'

Zan laughed and helped her off the couch. 'Perhaps he'll surprise you.'

'Perhaps.' Helen looked doubtful. 'So what happens now?'

'Everything is fine at the moment,' Carlo told her. 'I want you to go home and do as little as possible, which I realise is asking a great deal when you have two small children. If nothing happens then we see you again next week, but I have a suspicion that you might not be around to cook that turkey.'

'Well, I hope you're wrong.' Helen walked slowly to the door, one hand on her back to relieve the pressure.

Zan followed her out to the waiting room and Helen turned to her with a wicked smile.

'Where did you find him? He's totally gorgeous.' She buttoned up her coat and wound a scarf around her neck.

'I tell you this much, if he delivers my babies then I'll definitely know it's Christmas. I didn't think doctors could be that sexy.'

Zan managed a smile and walked with her towards the door. 'You shouldn't be thinking about sex at your stage, Helen.'

'Well, thinking is just about my only option,' Helen said gloomily, opening the door and shivering as the freezing air hit them both. 'And once these are born that'll be the end of it for ever.'

Zan laughed and gave her arm a squeeze. 'Have a good Christmas if I don't see you before.'

She walked back into the waiting room and gave herself a sharp talking-to. She'd known Carlo for less than twenty-four hours so she couldn't really feel anything for him. Not really. It was just because he was so different from the doctors she usually worked with.

Exotic, exciting—*Italian*.

It wasn't anything special about him.

Then she remembered the sexy look in his eyes, his gentle touch and the way he teased her, and she knew that her feelings had nothing to do with his nationality and everything to do with the man himself.

Carlo Bennett was special.

But he didn't want her.

She'd had her chance to spend the night with him and she'd blown it.

The clinic was hideously busy, and it was past two o'clock when Kim asked Zan to go to the labour ward.

'Vicky Morris has just come in and they reckon it's going to be the fastest delivery on record.'

Vicky was one of Zan's mothers and her face brightened. 'Oh, that's wonderful. She was desperate to be home before Christmas.'

Carlo frowned slightly. 'You haven't eaten lunch.'

'This is the NHS, Carlo,' Kim said dryly. 'What's lunch?'

'I'm not hungry anyway,' Zan said quickly, handing the last set of notes to Kim and making for the door. She was glad to get away from Carlo. 'I'll see you later.'

Up on the labour ward it was organised chaos, as usual.

'We've got two women labouring on the antenatal ward at the moment because we're full up here,' Diane told her as she gave Zan a quick hand-over. 'It looks as though your Vicky might deliver quickly, and frankly I hope she does because we need the space.'

'Always nice to work in such a relaxed environment,' Zan quipped, making her way along to Room 6.

She pushed open the door. 'Vicky, this is great—just what you wanted.'

'It doesn't feel great at the moment,' Vicky panted, her face white with pain. 'One minute I was Christmas shopping in town, minding my own business, and the next my waters break and suddenly I'm standing in a puddle in agony. I thought labour was supposed to be slow, but the midwife who admitted me told me that I'm already seven centimetres dilated.'

'And how are you coping?' Zan washed her hands and checked the CTG machine which provided a read-out of the baby's heartbeat and the mother's contractions.

'Well, all things considered, I'd rather be having lunch with the girls,' Vicky confessed, groaning as another pain hit her.

'Use the gas and air,' Zan instructed, encouraging Vicky to lift the mouthpiece. 'That's it. Well done.'

She put a hand on Vicky's abdomen and felt the strength of the contraction.

When it finally passed Vicky sagged back against the cushions, limp with exhaustion.

'OK, that's it. I've had enough. When can I go home?'

'Soon.' Zan gave her hand a squeeze. 'You need to start breathing in the gas and air at the beginning of the contraction. If you wait until it's really taken hold then there's no chance of it working.'

Vicky sighed. 'Nag, nag.'

'That's me.' Zan checked the foetal heart-rate and gave a nod. 'It's all looking good. Is the gas and air enough for you?'

'Well, I'd actually like a general anaesthetic,' Vicky said dryly, 'but I don't suppose that's on offer, is it?'

'Not today. Where's Andrew?'

Zan had met Vicky's husband at the last group of antenatal classes she'd run and knew that he was keen to be at the birth.

'He's on his way in. Oh, here we go again…' Vicky screwed up her face and started to breathe in the gas and air, her eyes tightly shut.

Zan encouraged her gently, watching the monitor to check that the baby's heart-rate wasn't affected by the contraction.

'I really, really want to push,' Vicky gasped, dropping the mouthpiece and grabbing the sides of the bed.

Zan frowned. Could she possibly have dilated that quickly?

'I just need to examine you again,' she said, washing her hands and dragging on a pair of sterile gloves. 'I don't want you pushing unless you're fully dilated.'

Two minutes later she looked at Vicky with a stunned expression on her face. 'Push away. You're obviously trying to do this in record time.'

She pressed the buzzer to summon some help and at that moment Andrew hurried into the room, looking out of breath and worried. Diane followed close behind him.

Vicky gave a sob of relief. 'I thought you weren't going to make it.'

'I didn't know you were planning to do it so quickly,' Andrew said, the strain evident in his face as he dropped his parcels by the door and went straight to his wife. 'You told me first labours always took hours.'

'Well, you know I like to be different.' Vicky gave another groan as another contraction hit her.

Zan encouraged her quietly and after several pushes the baby's head was delivered.

'The head's out now, Vicky,' Zan told her as she waited for the shoulders to rotate. 'Your baby will be born any minute.'

But the shoulders didn't rotate.

Feeling cold fingers of panic down her spine, Zan looked at Diane. 'I can't deliver the shoulders.' Zan kept her voice calm but both she and Diane understood the seriousness of the situation. Impacted shoulders were an obstetric emergency.

Vicky was breathing rapidly, dread showing in her eyes. 'What's the matter with the shoulders? Why can't you deliver them?'

'I'll fast-bleep the obstetrician,' Diane said immediately, and Zan turned her attention back to Vicky and her unborn baby.

'It will be all right,' she said quickly, praying that it was true. 'Sometimes the shoulders don't move into the right position and we have to give the baby some help.'

Diane reappeared only seconds later, accompanied by Carlo.

In the meantime Zan had made another attempt to deliver the shoulders and failed.

Zan looked at Carlo, her heart thumping in her chest. She knew just how serious the situation was. 'The anterior shoulder has failed to rotate. I've tried doing it manually, and I've checked that the hand isn't alongside the head.'

'So we'll try and deliver the posterior shoulder first.' He was amazingly calm, talking quietly to Vicky as he washed his hands and tugged on sterile gloves. 'Vicky, I need to change your position. The baby is stuck and we need to give him more room to be born.'

With Zan's help he adjusted Vicky's position and then he slipped his fingers behind the posterior shoulder and rotated it into the hollow of the sacrum.

Still talking quietly to Vicky, he did something magical with his fingers and the baby slithered out into his waiting hands. He lifted it straight onto Vicky's tummy.

Zan gave a gulp of relief and exchanged amazed looks with Diane, who grinned.

'Now I know it's Christmas. The time for miracles. Done that before, have you, Mr Bennett?'

'Not too often, fortunately.' Carlo smiled, his eyes on Vicky and the baby just as the paediatrician rushed in.

'Problems?'

Diane let out a long breath, not bothering to hide how thankful she was. 'Not any more—but now you're here you might as well check the baby.'

Carlo grabbed his coat and sprinted down the stairs to the front of the hospital.

Had he missed her?

He slammed through the main door and into the freezing air and then looked left and right, cursing the call from the ward that had slowed him down.

'Looking for someone?'

Her voice came from behind him and he turned, sighing with relief as he saw her standing there, dark hair pushed up inside her woolly hat again, her green eyes wary.

'I've been looking for you.'

For most of his adult life.

'Why's that?' Zan tried to sound casual but he could see the hurt in her eyes and he didn't blame her. He was only too aware that he was giving her mixed messages.

'I thought you were going to buy your tree.' He smiled down at her, remembering what she'd said the night before about getting a tree that would fill her flat. 'The *big* tree.'

'I am.' She stuffed her hands in her pockets and looked at him. 'Did I mention that you were great back there, by the way?' She rubbed her boot in the snow and avoided his eyes. 'You saved that baby's life. I'm impressed.'

So was he. He'd hurt her feelings but she was still generous enough to offer praise.

He took instant advantage. 'Impressed enough to cook me that dinner you promised me?'

He knew he shouldn't see her again, and he knew Matt was going to kill him, but he couldn't help himself. If Zan was a drug then he was well and truly hooked.

There was no way he was giving this girl up. He'd worry about the consequences later.

'I don't think so.' She turned to walk away from him and he grabbed her arm, his grip hard through the wool of her coat.

'If that Christmas tree is as big as you say then you're going to need help carrying it.'

She stared at him and shook her head. 'I'll be fine.'

'Zan.' He suddenly sounded very Italian and very frustrated. 'I meant what I said last night.'

She gave him a wan smile. 'You also made it perfectly clear in clinic this morning that you'd had second thoughts.'

He sucked in a deep breath but he didn't let her go. 'That isn't true.'

He'd been trying to do the right thing but he knew now

that he couldn't do that. He had to be with this woman and somehow he'd make sure that she was kept safe.

'I can read body language, Carlo.' She lifted her chin. 'So what did you want to talk about?'

'A relationship between us isn't straightforward.' He almost laughed as he listened to himself. That had to be the understatement of the year.

'You mean because you'll be going back to Italy?'

No. Because he was deceiving her about who he was. Because some crazed lunatic was out to get him.

'Zan—'

'I don't expect commitment,' she said, her head tipped to one side, her cheeks pink from the cold. 'All I want is for you to be honest with me.'

Carlo rubbed a hand over the back of his neck, her words creating an unbearable tension in his body.

Honest.

That was the one thing he wasn't being.

In many ways their whole relationship was a charade. She had absolutely no idea who she was involved with. What his life was like back in Italy.

And he ought to walk away from her but there was no way he could do it.

'Decorating a tree is no fun on your own.' *He'd make sure that she was kept safe,* he told himself. And he'd find a way to tell her the truth about himself when the time was right.

She looked at him for a long moment and he could see the question in her eyes.

She was trying to decide whether she could trust him.

'Should I buy a Scotch pine or a blue spruce?'

He grinned. 'Blue spruce. It's the best.'

CHAPTER FOUR

'IT's too big.' Carlo gazed up at the top of the Christmas tree and then back at Zan, who was winding the lights around the branches.

'It's not too big.' She crawled out from under the branches, eyes shining, humming along to the Christmas carols that were playing in the background.

'It's touching the ceiling,' Carlo pointed out, and she grinned.

'It's supposed to. Now we just have to decorate it.'

'We?' Carlo lifted an eyebrow and she nodded and handed him a box.

'Might as well make use of your superior height. These go on the top.'

He followed her instructions, trying not to be distracted by the way her jeans hugged her rounded bottom as she leaned over to hang things on the bottom of the tree.

He'd rushed things the night before and he'd made up his mind that he was going to control himself and slow the pace as he'd promised.

He just hoped he didn't die in the attempt.

He finished the top of the tree and then crouched down next to her to look through the rest of the decorations.

'We need to hang these at the front because they're so pretty.' She handed him a box of delicate silver baubles and he took them carefully, his fingers brushing against hers, their heads close together as they inspected the decorations.

'These *are* pretty.'

And so was she. Completely gorgeous. He was fascinated by those thick black lashes and the soft fullness of her mouth.

Carlo tilted his head so that their mouths were tantalisingly close and fought the urge to kiss her. He watched her lips part in anticipation and bit back a groan.

She wanted him to kiss her.

But he wasn't going to. He wanted to make sure that she was comfortable with him before he touched her again. And in the meantime he was going to make her want him as much as he wanted her.

Deliberately cranking up the heat, he hesitated just long enough to see her breathing quicken and then dragged his attention back to the baubles.

Every nerve ending in his body was tingling with frustration and he was grateful that he was wearing tailored trousers this time. At least they were slightly more forgiving than his jeans.

'So these go at the front?' Trying to keep his tone casual, he straightened up, still holding the box, and started hanging the baubles on the branches.

'Yes—just there—' she sounded breathless and he gritted his teeth, forcing himself not to turn round.

If he turned round he was going to kiss her, and he was determined not to kiss her again yet.

She wasn't touching him and yet every sense in his body alerted him to how close she was.

It occurred to him that he'd never been in this position before. He'd never had to hold back with a woman. But, then, the women he usually mixed with were experienced and sophisticated whereas Zan... He dragged in a breath and tried to ignore the way her subtle perfume wrapped itself around him. Zan was sweet and natural and she'd confessed that she had virtually no experience when it came to men.

The knowledge satisfied everything that was male in

him. She was going to be his and there was no way he was rushing her.

'Can you reach the plug to switch on the lights?' Her voice was husky and feminine and he clenched his fists and decided that he'd never known temptation before he'd met Zan.

'*Sì.*' He bent down and flicked the switch.

The tree lit up, throwing sparkling silver lights across her living room.

Zan gasped and clapped her hands. 'Oh, that's so pretty!' She smiled at him, her green eyes reflecting the glitter of a hundred tiny Christmas tree lights. 'Merry Christmas, Mr Bennett.'

The stark reminder that she didn't actually know who he was stabbed at his conscience. *She trusted him and he wasn't being honest with her.*

'It's very pretty.'

'Isn't it just?' She scrabbled in her bag and pulled out a piece of paper. 'I've just remembered. Lottery numbers for tomorrow. You can help me choose.'

He stared at her. She was expecting him to choose lottery numbers? He rubbed a hand over his jaw. 'Do you really want to do the lottery?'

In a few weeks, when all this was sorted out, he'd be able to buy her anything she wanted.

'Of course I want to do it. The jackpot is eleven million. *Eleven million.* Imagine how amazing it would be to win a bit of that at Christmas.' She grinned and sat cross-legged on the cushions which were always piled by the huge window. 'Go on, if you had all the money in the world what would you want from me as a present? It's got to be a car, right? You look like a man who likes fast cars.'

She was spot on. He did like fast cars. He already had three at home.

'Let me guess.' Zan tipped her head on one side and looked at him thoughtfully. 'Ferrari? Red?'

This was ridiculous.

'Ferrari, definitely.' He played along with her game, thinking how nice it was going to be to be able to buy her whatever she wanted.

'What else would you buy?'

Carlo stared at her, finding the whole situation surreal. Here was he, trying to pretend that he didn't have money, and she was asking him what he'd do if he did. It was enough to give a guy a headache.

Suddenly he realised just how much he took his life for granted. True, he was fed up with all the complications that went with wealth, but the benefits outweighed the disadvantages and he'd started to forget that.

'I'd buy a ski lodge,' he said slowly, thinking of their family home in Cortina, 'and a villa in Sardinia.'

In fact, all the things he already had. *And loved.*

'Sardinia?' She tipped her head on one side. 'Is that a nice place?'

'Fabulous.'

'Well, if we win, you're taking me there.' She sucked the pen and squinted at the numbers. 'I'll choose three and you choose three.'

Carlo suppressed a groan. He could just imagine the newspaper headlines if he won the lottery. They'd have a field day.

'You do it,' he suggested lightly. 'I don't want to bring you bad luck.'

Or at least he didn't want to bring her any more than he might already be bringing her.

She filled out the form, stuffed it back in her pocket and smiled at him. 'Remind me to take it to the newsagents later. Now, then, time for dinner.'

She cooked a fabulous chicken dish, bursting with flavour, and Carlo decided that he needed to find a way of getting her to ask him to stay at Christmas again. This time he'd say yes.

They dined by candlelight and Christmas tree lights and Carlo was just thinking that he couldn't remember a time when he'd been happier when she asked the question he'd been dreading.

'Tell me about your family.'

Carlo tensed. 'My family live in Milan,' he said carefully. 'My father owns his own business.'

And he was the richest man in Italy.

Zan tipped her head on one side and looked interested. 'What does he do?'

'Sort of medical supplies—technology,' Carlo hedged, hoping she wouldn't delve too deeply. His father's company was a household name in Europe and the States.

'But you weren't tempted to join him?'

'My brother and I wanted to carve our own way in the world,' Carlo told her, suddenly filled with an overwhelming desire to tell her just how hard it was to be the son of a billionaire. It was pretty hard to see yourself as successful when your father had success all sewn up.

'So your brother's a doctor, too? Where?'

'He works in Milan. He's a surgeon.' A famous children's heart surgeon, and she might even recognise the name if he mentioned it because he'd worked in her hospital for a while. Carlo chose not to mention it. 'He lives with his wife and their daughter, who's two now. They're expecting another baby any day. You're an amazing cook.'

'Well, someone had to help my mum and it certainly wasn't my brothers,' Zan said dryly, standing up and clearing the plates.

Carlo stood up, too, relieved that he appeared to have successfully changed the subject away from his family.

'I'll help you wash up.'

'No need; I've got a dishwasher.' She walked into the kitchen and opened a cupboard. 'This flat may be small but it's very well equipped. Can I ask you something?'

'Of course.' Carlo braced himself. Now what? More questions about his family that he was going to have to dodge?

She hesitated slightly. 'The children's ward is looking for someone to be Father Christmas. Usually the Chief Exec does it, because he's tall and broad and looks good in the outfit, but he's off sick with flu at the moment and...' She broke off and looked at him hopefully.

He grinned. She was *so* sweet. 'You want me to dress as Father Christmas?'

Her cheeks dimpled wickedly. 'I've always fancied men in uniform.'

'You have a fetish for men with white beards?'

They were both laughing and Carlo had to stop himself grabbing her. 'And where and when does all this take place?'

'The day after next. Christmas Eve. The children's ward opens onto a huge lawn so you arrive that way.'

'In my sledge?'

'Nothing so fancy, I'm afraid. This is the NHS. No sledges.' She closed the door of the dishwasher and pressed the button. 'You get to walk with a few elves as helpers to give out presents.'

Carlo looked at her thoughtfully, an idea forming in his mind.

'I'll do it,' he said immediately, and she gave him a wide smile that hit him straight in the solar plexus.

'That's great. You'll get to see my elf costume.'

If her elf costume was anywhere near as attractive as her tight jeans then the Father Christmas outfit had better be baggy.

Deciding that he'd stretched his self-control to the limits

for one night, he glanced at his watch and gave her a rueful smile.

'I'd better be going. Thanks for supper.'

'Thanks for helping with the tree.' She looked at him wistfully and then looked away quickly, but not before he'd caught the blush on her cheek.

He knew exactly what she wanted because he wanted the same thing and it was starting to drive him crazy.

'Zan...' His voice low, he reached out a hand and turned her face towards him, sliding his fingers around the back of her neck, feeling the softness of her dark hair teasing the back of his hand. 'So, after I've been Father Christmas, what happens then? Do the elves invite me home?'

She laughed. 'I think you spend the rest of the night squeezing yourself down chimneys.' Her laughter died and she looked at him warily. 'Alternatively, you could spend Christmas Eve here.' She gave a hesitant smile. 'But you didn't seem too wild about that idea when I mentioned it last night.'

Carlo stuck his hands in his pockets to stop himself grabbing her.

'Trust me, I'm wild about it.'

'Really?' She looked at him doubtfully and then smiled. 'In that case, we can come back here after our visit to the children's ward and then open presents on Christmas morning before we go to the hospital.'

Which meant that she was inviting him to stay the night.

His eyes gleamed in anticipation. 'Does that mean I get to hang my stocking next to yours?'

'That depends.' Zan gave a shy grin. 'Will it behave itself?'

'Probably not.' Carlo bent his head and brushed his mouth against hers in a kiss designed to tease and frustrate them both.

He had absolutely no intention of behaving himself.

Which meant that he had forty-eight hours to make sure she felt the same way.

'You're going to carry on seeing her?' Matt stared at him in dismay but Carlo merely grinned.

'I'm going to carry on seeing her, and you're going to protect her.' He almost laughed at the expression on Matt's face. 'Don't look like that. You're always dying to do your macho bodyguard act and here I am giving you permission. Be as macho as you like. Just don't let her see you.'

Matt exhaled sharply. 'Let's get this straight. You're asking me to follow the girl?'

'Absolutely,' Carlo said pleasantly. 'And her name is Zan.'

'I'm supposed to be protecting *you*.'

Carlo frowned impatiently. 'I protect myself. And anyway, apart from when I'm working I'm going to be with her, so protecting her will be protecting me.'

'You could be putting her in danger.'

'But you're the best,' Carlo said softly, 'and so am I. Between us we can stop anything happening to her. We have to, Matt, because there's no way I'm letting her go.'

'I can't believe you're doing this.' Matt raked long fingers through his cropped hair and his jaw tensed. 'Have you really thought this through? You're a multi-millionaire, Carlo. This can't be anything but a short-term relationship.'

'Why?' Carlo's tone was noticeably cooler and Matt glanced at him warily.

'You really need me to tell you that? You've got a life in Italy—your clinic is one of the most famous in the world. People pay huge sums of money to see you personally because you're so damn talented.'

'So maybe I want to use those talents with the less fortunate for a while,' Carlo replied smoothly, remembering what Zan had said about visiting Kelly. She made a difference.

'But sooner or later you'll be going back,' Matt pointed out logically. 'And then what?'

Carlo pushed the thought away. He didn't want to think about going back.

'I'll worry about that later. At the moment I just care about keeping her safe.'

And waking up next to her in bed on Christmas morning.

'And what if they use her to get to you?'

Carlo looked him in the eye. 'They're not going to do that.'

Matt frowned. 'And how can you be so sure?'

'Because we're going to be protecting her,' Carlo said smoothly. 'I don't want her to go anywhere without one of us within hugging distance of her.'

Matt blinked. 'You seriously want me to tail your girlfriend?'

'I want you to do whatever it takes to keep her safe,' Carlo said gruffly. 'You're the best. We both know that. No one gets past you.'

'Which is why I'm supposed to be looking after you,' Matt said dryly, his frustration obvious. 'What's it going to do for my professional reputation if they get you?'

'They won't,' Carlo said calmly. 'You know as well as I do that I can take care of myself. We also both know that I shouldn't be dragging Zan into this, but I have, so now it's my responsibility to keep her safe. I want you on her tail every time she leaves that flat of hers and I want you or one of the team parked outside her apartment every night. No one enters or leaves without your knowledge. Oh, and by the way...' Carlo gave a smug grin. 'She's invited me to spend Christmas with her so I'll be staying with her on Christmas Eve.'

Matt shook his head. 'You've lost your marbles.'

'You only think that because you haven't seen her,' Carlo drawled, shrugging out of his coat and walking towards his bedroom.

'And are you going to tell her the truth?'

Carlo stopped walking. 'No. Not yet.'

He was enjoying the simplicity of their relationship.

'And what if she goes to the press once she finds out who you are?'

Carlo's fingers tightened on his coat. 'Then I'll have made a serious error of judgement.'

Carlo hadn't laid a finger on her.

Zan pulled her coat over her uniform the next morning and tried to squash the feelings of disappointment.

They'd spent the whole evening together and he hadn't even kissed her properly. About a dozen times she'd thought he was going to—at one point he'd seemed to be within kissing distance every time she'd turned around—but he hadn't made that final move. Obviously he wasn't as frustrated as she was. She was beginning to wish she hadn't said no on the first night.

She'd wanted him to slow down, not stop altogether!

She stepped out of the lift and through the door that led to the street, gasping as the cold hit her. It had stopped snowing but the air was freezing and her breath made smoky clouds ahead of her as she hurried along the pavement towards the hospital.

It was still fairly early but the roads were already busy and there were several other people walking to work, heads down against the cold.

Uneasy after her experience with the muggers, Zan glanced briefly over her shoulder, checking that no one was following her. The only person behind her was an elderly woman with a stick and on the other side of the road a broad-shouldered man in a long coat strode briskly, paying no attention to her whatsoever.

She relaxed slightly but still felt considerable relief when she reached the hospital gates and hurried inside.

The unit was as busy as ever and Zan made her way to the antenatal clinic.

Kim was looking harassed. 'Just tell me, what happened nine months ago?'

Zan dragged the scarf off her neck and raised an eyebrow. 'Frankly, I have trouble remembering what happened yesterday. Why are you asking about nine months ago?'

'Because I want to know why there are so many women delivering this week,' Kim muttered, staggering under the weight of a pile of notes that she was carrying back to the desk. 'Did I miss a wild party or something? I'm trying to count back and work it out.'

Zan laughed. 'Don't be a misery. Christmas babies are always really special. I'm still hoping that Helen will have her twins on Christmas Day.'

Kim gave her an incredulous look. 'Don't you want to eat your turkey in peace?'

Zan gave a wistful smile. 'I just think it would be really exciting if the twins were born on Christmas Day.'

'You need your head examined.' Kim glanced up with a smile as a very pregnant woman approached the desk. 'Hello, Millie. How have you been?'

Zan picked up the first set of notes and walked through to her consulting room to begin the clinic.

She saw a steady stream of patients and it was lunchtime before she caught up with Kim again.

'Are you joining me in the canteen for lunch?' Kim's eyes gleamed with curiosity. 'I want to hear episode two of your story.'

Episode two had been decidedly non-eventful, Zan reflected gloomily. Lots of tension but absolutely no action. Carlo hadn't even kissed her. Apart from the brief touch of his lips when he'd left her for the night. And that hadn't really been a kiss. More a tease.

She gave a slow smile as a suspicion grew in her mind.

Was he playing games with her?

Was he trying to drive her wild?

Maybe that was exactly what he was trying to do.

Suddenly cheered, she smiled at Kim. 'I'm popping out at lunchtime to buy a present for my brother.' It was true. She still had a couple more things to buy. 'But I'm still free tonight for that pizza.'

She and Kim had arranged to go out the previous week and she'd been looking forward to it.

Having arranged the details, she wrapped up warmly, slipped out of the hospital and walked towards the shops.

The streets were crowded with Christmas shoppers loaded with bags and she fought her way into a small boutique that sold unusual knitwear and chose a chunky ribbed jumper for her brother.

Then she remembered Carlo. If he was spending Christmas with her then she'd need to buy him something.

Thinking back to their conversation, she smiled.

She knew exactly what to buy him and she knew just the shop.

She was hovering by the till, waiting to pay, when she glanced up and noticed a man buying chestnuts across the road.

It was the same man that she'd seen that morning.

Frowning slightly, Zan paid for the jumper, trying to convince herself that it was perfectly possible to bump into the same person twice in one morning. He probably worked locally.

She was just jumpy after the attack the night before.

Still feeling edgy, she left the shop and went back to

the hospital, telling herself that there was nothing to worry about.

Kim grabbed her as soon as she arrived back in the clinic.

'Someone called for you but they didn't leave their name. It was a woman and she sounded frantic.'

Zan dumped her parcels and frowned. Who would have called her?

Her eyes widened as a thought struck her. 'Kelly?'

'Possibly.' Kim gave a sigh. 'I did ask her, but she hung up at that point.'

'Oh, help.' Zan glanced round the packed clinic and bit her lip. 'Do you think…?'

'Maybe. You'd better check it out,' Kim said immediately. 'I'll call the agency and see if I can get some extra help here. If you need anything, call us. Not that she's likely to let anyone help but you.'

Without waiting to argue, Zan sprinted off and found the bag she used for community visits. She checked the contents, added some extra equipment and then made her way to the door.

For a brief moment she contemplated telling Carlo where she was going and then she thought better of it.

He was busy in the clinic and she didn't want to interrupt him.

Carlo had just finished seeing a patient when his mobile rang.

It was Matt.

Carlo listened in silence and then closed his eyes briefly, his broad shoulders suddenly tense. 'She's gone into the flat?'

He listened to Matt's response and then let out a long breath. 'Hang around outside. I'll be there in ten minutes.'

He made two more phone calls and then snapped the

phone shut and went to find Kim, who was placating a woman who'd been waiting for two hours.

'We have a problem.' He took her to one side and glanced around to check that no one was within earshot. 'Zan's with Kelly and I think she needs help.'

Kim's eyes widened. 'She's called you?'

'I...er...yes.'

No. His bodyguard had been following her. And he'd heard a woman screaming from inside the flat.

Had it been Kelly or Zan?

Sweat broke out on his brow.

The temptation to order Matt to break the door down had been overwhelming.

'Oh, hell.' Kim raked fingers through her blonde hair, visibly panicking. 'I shouldn't have let Zan go on her own, but the problem is that the husband won't let anyone else near her.'

'I'm going to see if I can help her.'

Kim shook her head. 'They won't let you in.'

'They might.' *They'd let him in before.* Just. 'The registrar can cover the rest of the clinic. If he has a problem he can call me.'

Kim nodded and looked at him helplessly. 'What can I do to help?'

'Nothing for now.' Carlo dragged on his coat and picked up his bag. Then he paused. 'On second thoughts, maybe you can. Do you have a portable oxygen cylinder?'

'I'll fetch it.' Obviously thinking along the same lines, they hurried to the equipment room.

Carlo stuffed a bag full of equipment while Kim helped.

'I really, really hope you don't need any of this,' she said fervently, and he nodded agreement.

'Let's hope not. But if that baby is arriving six weeks prematurely, in a freezing flat, we could have a problem on our hands.'

It was an understatement, and they both knew it.

Kim walked with him to the door. 'I'll alert Social Services and the ambulance service. If necessary, we can put an incubator in the ambulance.'

'Good. I'll call you.' Carlo strode out of the door and made for the car park.

Slumped in a car at the far end of the car park, two men watched as Carlo walked towards his car. The bigger of the two men sat up slightly, suddenly alert, checking a photograph that lay in his lap.

'That's him.'

His partner nodded agreement and both of them watched while Carlo slid into the driver's seat and drove away.

'So we've finally tracked him down. Now what?'

'Nothing yet.' The man gave an unpleasant smile. 'We wait. But Carlo Santini is about to have a memorable Christmas.'

CHAPTER FIVE

ZAN finished examining Kelly for the second time and tried to stay calm.

It was the hardest thing she'd ever done.

The flat was freezing and she was delivering a premature baby at home.

This was a midwife's equivalent of a bad hair day.

'Kelly, you have to let me call an ambulance,' she said quietly as she listened to the foetal heart again. So far it had been steady and strong, but it was starting to dip with contractions and Zan was feeling vulnerable and exposed with so little equipment and no medical back-up.

Mike stepped forward, his eyes cold. 'She has the baby here.'

Zan glanced at Kelly but she just stared at the floor, her face white with pain, her long hair straggly as it hung past her thin shoulders.

For a wild moment Zan wondered whether she could floor Mike and drag Kelly bodily to hospital.

But that wasn't an option, of course.

She was just going to have to do the best she could in the circumstances.

'Just as long as you realise that this baby is going to be very small when it's born,' Zan told him. 'Babies born this early often need to go to our intensive care unit to help them breathe.'

Kelly gave a little sob and bent double as another pain hit her.

Zan talked to her quietly, reminding her how to breathe,

almost wishing that Kelly had bonded with another midwife.

Why her?

Kelly gave a sharp scream and even though the room was freezing Zan felt sweat break out on her forehead.

'Try and remember your breathing, Kelly,' she murmured gently, rubbing the other girl's back, horrified by how thin she was.

'I want to push,' Kelly sobbed, and Zan examined her again to check that her cervix was fully dilated.

'You're right,' she said finally, 'you are ready to push. Let's get you into a better position.'

She glanced at Mike, but before she could speak there was a loud knocking at the door.

Mike glared at her threateningly. 'Did you call someone?'

'You've been in the room with me the whole time,' Zan pointed out logically, 'so you know I haven't.'

'Then who——?'

'Mike, it's Carlo Bennett.' Carlo's deep voice penetrated the door and Zan closed her eyes in relief.

Kim must have told him.

Mike's mouth tightened. 'I'll get rid of him.'

'No!' Zan's sharp tone stopped him as he strode towards the door, shoulders braced for conflict.

'He ain't coming near my Kelly!'

Zan took a deep breath. 'Mike, ideally Kelly should be in hospital, but if you won't allow that then at least let the doctor come to her. *Please.*'

Mike's jaw was set. 'No way.'

'Mike, *please.*' Kelly spoke in a quivering voice and then gave a groan as she pushed again.

Mike looked at her uncertainly. 'No…'

'Let him in,' Kelly whispered, her eyes squeezed tightly shut and her hand gripping Zan's.

Without another word Mike dragged open the door and Zan felt the tension drain out of her as she saw Carlo, broad-shouldered and powerful, standing in the doorway with an impressive array of equipment tucked under his arm.

'Thank goodness.' Zan shot him a look of pure relief and he gave her a reassuring smile.

'It'll be OK.' He put a hand on Mike's shoulder, ignoring the frosty look that the other man gave him. 'Can I take a look at her?'

Mike hesitated, but then glanced at Kelly again and stood to one side.

Carlo found the bathroom, washed his hands and then crouched down beside Zan.

'How are you doing, Kelly?'

'Not too good.' The girl was deathly pale and clearly exhausted.

'Her waters broke in the night but she didn't call until lunchtime,' Zan told him. 'I've tried to persuade them to go to the hospital but they won't. She's fully dilated and ready to push.'

'So hospital isn't an option for the moment,' Carlo muttered, glancing around him with a frown. 'This place is too cold for a premature baby.'

Without waiting for an answer from anyone, he reached into his pocket for his mobile phone, leaving Zan to deal with Kelly.

'I'm just calling a friend,' he told Mike, and proceeded to dial a number and speak in rapid Italian.

Zan had no idea what he was doing. She was too busy delivering the baby.

She'd brought clean sheets and blankets from the hospital, and she laid them out now and fished the mucus extractor out of her bag.

Then she prepared an injection to give Kelly to help her uterus contract once the baby had been born.

'I'll give that.' Slipping the phone back into his pocket, Carlo took the syringe from her and watched while Zan delivered the baby's head.

'Gently now, Kelly,' she said quietly as she controlled the delivery. 'That's great...'

As the head slid out Zan felt her heart start to pound. The baby was so tiny. It should have been born in hospital, with a team of paediatricians handy and a warm intensive-care cot ready.

Instead, it was about to be born in a filthy flat which was freezing cold, while snow fell outside.

Kelly gasped as another contraction hit her and Zan delivered the anterior shoulder, aware that Carlo had swiftly given the necessary injection and was now preparing himself to take the baby.

'You see to the mother,' he ordered quietly, and as the baby slithered into her waiting hands she found herself praying.

'You have a little boy, Kelly,' she said softly, passing the limp body to Carlo, who wrapped the baby in a towel.

Please, let him cry.

The baby lay still, showing no signs of life. His skin was tinged a sickly blue colour and he made no effort to breathe.

Kelly struggled upright and then gave a sob of desperation. 'Why isn't he crying? *Why isn't he crying?*'

Zan bit her lip and tried to keep her voice steady. 'Mr Bennett's just examining him, Kelly.'

Kelly's eyes were wild and she shook her head. 'No! Oh, my God, no—tell me he isn't—'

'We're working on it, Kelly,' Carlo was using the mucus extractor to clear the airway but he glanced up when he heard the knock on the door.

'Open it,' he ordered harshly. Mike heard the command in his tone and for once responded without argument.

Zan's eyes widened as he came back into the room carrying two heaters.

Following Carlo's instructions, Mike plugged the heaters in and positioned them.

Heat belted into the room and Carlo dried the baby carefully and reached for the oxygen. Then he directed a low flow of oxygen over the baby's face to try and stimulate a gasp reflex.

Meanwhile Zan turned her attention back to Kelly and delivered the placenta.

Despite her weakened state, Kelly seemed to be doing remarkably well, but she was obviously beside herself with worry about the baby.

'Please, don't let him die—*please*. Oh, Mike—do something.'

Tearing sobs shook her slight frame and Zan put her arms around her, praying for a miracle.

It was Christmas. Didn't miracles happen at Christmas? Obviously not.

The baby was limp and unresponsive and Mike gave a moan of anguish, the fight draining out of him.

Zan felt her eyes fill.

It was so unfair.

The baby was so tiny and helpless.

It deserved to live.

Finally Carlo bent his head and covered the baby's mouth and nose with his mouth, breathing gently. Then he started cardiac massage, using his index and middle fingers to depress the sternum.

The tears spilled out of Zan's eyes and trickled down her cheeks. Maybe it was unprofessional to cry but she just couldn't help it.

She could see that Carlo was using every trick at his disposal but the baby was showing no signs of responding. He was just too little.

'What's happening—?' Mike's voice was rough with panic and Zan looked at him pleadingly, trying to appeal to the father in him.

'He's very, very sick. We have to get the baby to hospital. Please, let me call an ambulance. *Please*, Mike…' She choked slightly and saw Mike hesitate, but before he could speak the baby gave a little cough and a feeble cry.

Kelly gasped in delight. 'He's alive! You've done it. Oh, thank you.' She burst into tears again and Mike frowned and went to put his arms around her.

Carlo was still working on the baby.

'He isn't out of the woods yet,' he said grimly, wrapping the baby warmly and covering his head to prevent further heat loss. 'This baby is tiny, Kelly, and he's grunting. That means that he's having trouble with his lungs. Babies that are born early can suffer from something called respiratory distress syndrome. They need help with their breathing.'

'And what happens if they don't get it?' Kelly's voice shook and Carlo looked directly at Mike.

'Sometimes they die.'

Zan flinched at the brutality of his words but she knew what he was trying to do. He was trying to make Mike understand the seriousness of the situation. Carlo had produced a miracle but this baby was desperately in need of hospital care, and without it…

Kelly turned to Mike, her eyes terrified. 'We have to let them take him into hospital. *We have to!*'

Mike was breathing heavily. 'You know how I feel about hospitals.'

'I know.' Tears were streaming down Kelly's face as she watched Carlo working to save her son. 'And I wanted to stay at home, too. But that's before it all went wrong.

He's ill, Mike. If he stays at home he might die, and we'll always blame ourselves and I don't think I can live with that. They're trying to help. They *care*. They're not like the others.'

'What others?' Carlo asked the question, still monitoring the baby's breathing.

Zan held her breath. In the few months she'd been coming to visit them she'd never got to the bottom of Kelly's story. All she knew was what the social worker had told her. That Kelly and Mike hated doctors and hospitals.

No one knew why.

'If you can tell us what happened, what you're so afraid of, then maybe we can help,' she said softly, and Kelly swallowed hard.

'Mike lost his brother...' She glanced nervously at Mike, obviously expecting her confession to provoke an angry reaction, but Mike was slouched against the wall, his face drawn.

Carlo looked up, his gaze suddenly intent. 'I'm sorry. That must have been terrible for you. What happened?'

'Doctors. That's what happened,' Mike answered bitterly. 'Eddie found a lump in his testicle but his GP kept telling him it was nothing. By the time he found out how serious it was he had just a few weeks to live.'

Kelly reached out a hand but Mike turned away and strode into the kitchen, slamming the door behind him.

Kelly flinched and looked at them helplessly. 'He adored Eddie. They were twins. When he lost him I thought...' She broke off and looked at the closed door with something close to desperation in her eyes. 'I thought I'd lose Mike, too. We've been going through a terrible patch. He never lets me out of his sight. He says I'm all he has now and he doesn't want to put me in anyone's care.'

Carlo let out a breath, visibly moved.

'I can understand that. In the same circumstances I wouldn't be that eager to trust the medical profession either.' Carlo rose to his feet and glanced at Zan. 'Try and get the baby on the breast. His blood sugar is low and he needs food. If his breathing changes, call me. I'm going to talk to Mike.'

He opened the kitchen door and closed it behind him, and Zan lifted the baby, positioning him against Kelly's breast, trying to encourage him to feed.

The baby played idly with the nipple but showed no inclination to suck.

Kelly gave a sob of desperation. 'He can't do it,' she wailed, and Zan frowned, determined not to give up.

'He's very little,' she said quietly. 'His suck reflex may not be fully developed yet. We'll just persevere.'

She also suspected that Kelly's poor physical condition might limit her supply of milk, but now wasn't the time to discuss that.

There was no other way of getting food into the baby in this tiny flat. He desperately needed to be in Special Care, with high-tech equipment and a specialised medical team.

At least Carlo's heaters had warmed the place up.

Even as she held the baby in place for another try, Carlo and Mike came out of the kitchen and Carlo reached for his phone.

'We're taking you both to hospital,' he said gruffly, his voice heavily accented and lines of strain visible around his dark eyes. 'Mike's agreed it's the best thing.'

'Oh, Mike…' Kelly burst into tears again and Zan gave a sigh of relief.

She just hoped it wouldn't be too late for the baby.

Carlo was talking into his phone and within minutes an ambulance crew were at the door.

Only moments later the baby was in the warm incubator

inside the ambulance and Mike and Kelly were seated next to her.

Zan looked at Carlo in amazement. 'How did you arrange all that so quickly?'

'I didn't.' He flashed her a smile and sprang into the ambulance after the crew. 'I arranged it all before I left. They've been parked at the end of the road, waiting for my call.'

Zan was stunned. 'But Mike might have refused...'

'I have amazing powers of persuasion.' He lowered his voice and gave her a sexy smile. 'You'd do well to remember that, Suzannah.'

Zan followed the ambulance in her car and once back at the hospital the whole team moved into action.

The baby was taken to the special care baby unit and Kelly was taken to the ward for a check-up and a rest.

'But I want to see the baby,' she fretted, as they examined her again.

'As soon as the paediatric staff ring us, we'll take you up to the special care baby unit,' Zan promised. 'They're just taking a good look at him and deciding what he needs.'

Mike was hovering nearby, not knowing whether to worry more about his wife or his son.

Carlo had gone straight up with the baby and the ambulance crew and was supervising the hand-over.

Zan was only too aware that the baby was alive only because of him and she was totally in awe of his skills as a doctor.

He was incredible.

She didn't know a single other doctor who would have coped in that situation. The flat had been filthy and freezing and he'd had next to no equipment. But he'd managed to resuscitate the baby and keep it alive until he could talk sense into the father and transfer the family to hospital.

And he'd been *so* cool.

Finally SCBU rang to say that they were ready for the parents, and Zan took Kelly and Mike up to see their son.

'It can seem a bit scary when you first see him,' she warned, knowing that the baby would be having a lot of help. 'He might have tubes in to help him breathe and things.'

'I don't care.' Kelly gave a gulp and clung to Mike's hand. 'As long as he's alive, I don't care.'

Mike was white with the strain and there was no sign of his usually tough approach to life.

It was much later, after mother and baby had been re-united and she was back on the labour ward, that Zan suddenly remembered that she'd caught a glimpse of a man watching her before she'd knocked on Kelly's door.

He was the same man she'd seen on her way to work and then again when she'd been shopping for Christmas presents.

Zan shifted uneasily.

Was she imagining it?

'Why are you frowning?' Carlo's deep voice came from directly in front of her and she gave a start.

She'd been so deep in thought that she hadn't even seen him approach.

'Oh—hi.' She smiled at him. 'Have you finished on SCBU?'

He nodded, his smile weary. 'Now we just have to hope the little chap makes it.'

'You were amazing.' Her voice was soft. 'I don't know what I would have done if you hadn't arrived. The baby would have died, Carlo.'

'Maybe not.'

He seemed oblivious to his accomplishment but Zan was under no illusions. She knew that he'd saved that baby.

'So, come on, why were you looking so worried a minute ago?' His eyes narrowed and he looked at her searchingly. 'Tell me.'

She blushed. What if she'd imagined it all? 'I'm probably being stupid…'

'But?' he prompted her gently, and she bit her lip.

'I think someone is following me. I saw this man this morning on my way to work, and then again at lunchtime when I did some shopping, and when I arrived at Kelly's flat—' She broke off, aware that Carlo was suddenly looking tense.

'Can you describe him?'

Zan looked at him, surprised by the urgency in his tone. 'I don't know…' She racked her brains. 'Tall, broad, dark hair—he wore a fawn coat with a black scarf…'

Carlo seemed to relax. 'I'm sure it was your imagination,' he said lightly, and she gave him an odd look.

'I saw him, Carlo.'

'I don't doubt that you saw him,' he replied smoothly, 'but I'm sure it was your imagination that he was following you. Maybe he was just going to the same places as you.'

Zan frowned. That might explain the first two encounters, but what would he have been doing outside Kelly's flat?

Still, Carlo obviously didn't think there was anything to worry about, and maybe he was right. It wasn't as if the man had shown any interest in her after all. He hadn't even been looking in her direction.

'It's been a long day.' Carlo seemed keen to change the subject. 'I'm on call but everything seems quiet at the moment so can I buy you supper?'

Zan smiled. 'I'm meeting Kim for a pizza at our favourite Italian restaurant. I didn't think you'd be free.'

'I'm free until I get called out.' Carlo said immediately. 'I'm feeling hideously homesick and I could do with some Italian cooking. You have to invite me.'

'Invite you where?' Kim bounced up to them, a brightly coloured scarf wrapped around her neck. 'Are you joining us?'

'Is that OK?'

'Of course.' Kim grinned at him and then glanced at Zan, who was bright pink. Her mouth fell open. 'Oh, my goodness—how could I be so slow? You're the one who—'

'Kim!' Zan interrupted her before she could say something indiscreet, and Carlo smiled.

'Why don't we go and eat? I'm starving.'

The restaurant was tucked away in a back street and the welcoming heat hit them as soon as they opened the door.

The owner greeted them in Italian and almost dropped the plates he was carrying when Carlo replied equally fluently.

Delighted to have a customer who spoke his language, the owner was immediately distracted and talked for several minutes before finding them a table.

Carlo ordered some wine and sat back in his chair while they all looked at the menu.

'So how did you two meet?' Kim was showing no interest in the idea of food.

Zan shrank into her chair in embarrassment. 'Kim, we're not—'

'Yes, we are.' Carlo's voice was firm and he flashed her a reassuring smile before turning his attention to Kim. 'We fell over each other in the street while she was on her way to visit Kelly. I didn't think it was a great place for a girl to be wandering on her own so I went with her. Then we had dinner last night.'

Zan's face heated under the look he gave her. She couldn't quite believe that this man wanted her.

She didn't need to notice that all the women in the restaurant were sneaking looks at him to be aware of his attractions. He was gorgeous. Warm and charismatic, but incredibly strong, too.

It was a combination that left her breathless.

'Well, you've definitely got the touch,' Kim said dryly, picking up the bottle of wine and helping herself. 'Have you any idea how many men Zan's chased away over the years?'

Zan flushed with embarrassment. 'Carlo's agreed to be Father Christmas,' she said quickly, changing the subject before Kim said something to embarrass her further.

Kim grinned. 'Really? You wait until you see Zan in her elf costume. Father Christmas usually has trouble with his blood pressure from the moment she takes off her coat. I keep a supply of suitable drugs at the ready.'

Their order arrived and they ate their meal, talking and laughing, and it was only when she glanced up to order coffee that Zan noticed the man sitting on his own at a table in the corner of the restaurant.

She gave a gasp and the colour drained from her face.

'What?' Kim looked at her in alarm. 'What's the matter?'

Carlo frowned. 'Zan?'

She reached across the table and grabbed his hand. 'It's the same man I saw earlier,' she whispered urgently. 'He's sitting at the table by the window. It can't be a coincidence. Every where I go, he's there, too.'

Carlo glanced around and then turned his attention back to the table as the waiter brought the coffee.

'Just ignore him,' he advised, but his fingers tightened on hers reassuringly.

Zan bit her lip. What was the matter with her? She was behaving like a real baby.

'Sorry.' She gave him a wan smile. 'I'm being stupid, aren't I? I've never really been nervous of anything before. But after the other night I'm a bit jumpy.'

Kim frowned. 'What happened the other night?'

Carlo was looking at Zan, his expression reassuring. 'There's no need to be jumpy, *cara mia*. No one is going to hurt you.' There was a hint of steel under his warm, male tones. 'We will drink our coffee and then I will take you back to your flat myself.'

She loved the fact that he was so protective.

Glancing at his powerful shoulders, she suddenly had a disturbing memory of him naked in the shower and, remembering his raw, male sexuality, she felt excitement spiral up through her body. He had an incredible physique. It was hardly surprising that he wasn't intimidated by anyone.

'Will someone please tell me what's going on?' Kim glanced between them with a mixture of concern and frustration.

'Someone attacked me the other night,' Zan said flatly. 'Carlo rescued me. It's how we met.'

Kim stared at her in horror. 'Someone *attacked* you?' She lifted a hand to her mouth. 'Oh, my God! Were you hurt?'

Zan shrugged and shook her head. 'Not really.'

Kim looked at Carlo in dismay. 'And your eye—is that how…?'

Carlo laughed. 'No. That was Zan. She was fighting like a wildcat when I got to her. She mixed me up with the attackers.'

Kim blinked in disbelief. 'And what were you saying about someone following you?'

Zan put down her coffee-cup and glanced across the

restaurant again. 'Every time I turn around, that man is behind me.' She lifted her chin and frowned. 'In fact, I'm going to stop being so pathetic and confront him. I want to know why he's following me.'

She rose to her feet but Carlo put a hand on her arm.

'Sit down.' His voice was calm but firm. 'Finish your coffee. I'll deal with it.'

She opened her mouth to argue and then closed it again, seeing the sense in his suggestion.

After all, if the man following her realised that she was with Carlo then he might think twice about following her.

Carlo strode over to Matt and sat down in a vacant seat, his back to the two women.

'You're losing your touch,' Carlo told Matt grimly, his brows locked together in a frown. 'She knows you're following her.'

'I guessed as much.' Matt rubbed a hand over his jaw and looked apologetic. 'Sorry. I underestimated her. The girl's been looking over her shoulder every two minutes and frankly I didn't expect her to be so jumpy.'

'Nor me.' Carlo felt his insides twist. He hated to think that Zan was frightened. She'd successfully concealed the fact from him.

'Whatever happened the other night obviously freaked her out,' Matt said thoughtfully. 'On her way to work this morning she looked over her shoulder at least eight times and she didn't slow down until she walked inside those hospital gates. She was better at lunchtime but she was still keeping an eye on her surroundings. She dashed to Kelly's house so quickly I didn't realise she'd seen me.'

'Damn.' Carlo was frowning but Matt gave a shrug.

'Actually, I think it's probably a good thing that she's alert in the circumstances.'

'Alert, maybe, but I don't want her frightened,' Carlo growled. 'I hadn't even noticed that she was nervous.'

Matt shrugged. 'She probably isn't when she's with you. It's just when she's on her own.'

'Well, you're going to have to keep a low profile now,' Carlo pointed out, dragging his fingers through his hair and letting out a long sigh. 'Maybe we'd better get one of the other guys to follow her.'

Matt lifted an eyebrow and Carlo shook his head. 'No, you're right. Bad idea. At least I know that if she's with you nothing's going to happen to her. Maybe I should tell her the truth.'

The longer it went on, the worse he felt about the fact he was deceiving her and he knew he was going to be faced with a major dilemma soon.

Could he make love to a woman who didn't know who he was?

'You can't tell her!' Matt glared at him. 'Not until we've caught those lunatics. You don't know that you can trust her.'

'But if she sees you again...'

'She won't. I'll be invisible and I'll change my image tomorrow.'

'All right.' Carlo was still disturbed by the news that Zan was so nervous. Why hadn't she told him? 'Oh, and by the way, while we're working in the hospital and you're kicking your heels, I need you to do something for me.'

Matt's eyes narrowed warily. 'I hardly dare ask.'

'I need you to find me a team of reindeer and a sleigh.'

Matt blinked. 'Reindeer.' His tone was faint. 'And a *sleigh*?'

'That's right. I'm going to be Father Christmas.'

And he was going to give Zan a Christmas to remember.

He walked back to the table and gestured to the waiter to bring the bill.

'It's fine, *tesoro*,' he said easily, paying the waiter in cash and reaching for his coat. 'If you saw him earlier then I'm sure it was just coincidence. He's Italian and he lives around here.'

She accepted what he said without argument and he felt a pang of guilt as he saw the trusting look in her eyes.

Whatever happened, he was going to keep her safe.

They said goodnight to Kim and then made their way back to Zan's flat.

'Only two more days until Christmas.' She smiled at him, her cheeks pink from the cold. 'Do you want to come up?'

Yes. He wanted to check that her flat was safe.

'I'll just see you into your flat and then I'd better go home.' He followed her into the lift and waited while she found her keys, his senses constantly alert to danger.

'Why do you keep looking around you?' She looked at him anxiously and this time he sensed her nerves. 'I thought you said that man wasn't following me.'

Damn. She was amazingly observant.

'He's not,' he said smoothly, cursing the fact that Matt hadn't been more discreet. It was going to be harder to keep a careful watch on Zan from now on.

Carlo took her keys and unlocked the door, hoping that she'd think he was chivalrous by nature. The truth was he wanted to enter her flat first.

He wasn't taking any chances.

He flicked on the lights and glanced swiftly around the room. Everything was neat and ordered. No sign of problems.

She tilted her head to one side and smiled. 'Coffee?'

'I shouldn't.' He walked towards her window and gazed

down at the river below with a frown. The view was great but he wished she had curtains. From the outside this room would be lit up like a stage. 'I've got to go home and practise being Father Christmas in front of my mirror.'

And tighten the security arrangements so that she was kept safe.

He wanted someone to check the opposite bank of the river to see just how visible her flat was.

'I haven't had a chance to thank you for this afternoon,' Zan blurted out. 'If it hadn't been for you, I dread to think what would have happened to Kelly and the baby. It's lucky Kim told you I was there.'

Kim hadn't told him, but he wasn't in a position to correct her.

'Resuscitating a baby in those surroundings was certainly a new experience,' he admitted dryly, and she shook her head in admiration.

'So you mostly dealt with infertility in your last job?'

'Actually, we offered a total care package,' he explained. 'From conception to discharge home after delivery.'

'Do you think the baby will be all right?'

He pulled a face and shrugged. 'Who can say? He's in the right place now—all we can do is wait and see. I'm just glad they agreed to go to hospital in the end. It made life a lot easier.'

She nodded agreement and smiled up at him. Suddenly the smile faltered and her green eyes locked with his, anticipation heating her gaze.

She wanted him to kiss her.

The silence thickened around them and he sucked in a breath.

'I'd better go.' His voice came out in a croak and he

almost laughed at himself. He'd never been so clumsy around a woman before.

But, then, he'd never known chemistry like this before either. The sexual tension between them was so powerful that it was a living force, drawing them together.

She stepped closer to him, her eyes never leaving his.

'Do you want to go?' Her question was loaded with meaning and he closed his eyes briefly.

How had he ever got himself in this mess?

He couldn't make love to her when she didn't even know who he was. He just couldn't do it.

'Zan, I don't think—'

She reached up and touched a finger to his mouth, silencing him.

'That first night, when you wanted to make love, it just felt a bit fast.' Her slim fingers were locked on the front of his jumper, hanging onto him, her eyes incredibly shy. 'But you're not a stranger any more and I— I mean, if you still want to…'

Her meaning was clear and he felt desire slam through his body.

She wanted him to make love to her because she felt that she was beginning to know him.

But she didn't know him.

He wasn't who he said he was. In fact, she knew virtually nothing about him.

Conscience ripped through him and he muttered a curse and stepped back from her.

Having a secret identity had been great at the beginning, but it had gone from being the solution to the problem.

Her hands fell to her sides and she wrapped her arms around her middle self-consciously. 'You've changed your mind.' She kept her tone light and her brave smile made him want to thump the wall.

'I haven't changed my mind.' His voice was husky and he fought the urge to reach for her again. 'I promised you I'd slow the pace.'

'Oh.' Zan's eyes brightened and the smile that followed his confession was pure sexual invitation.

Heat engulfed his body.

For a woman with no experience she certainly knew how to make a man sweat.

She licked her lips. 'You need to learn the difference between slow and stop.' Her eyes dropped to his mouth and then lifted to his eyes.

Drawn in by the expression in her green eyes, Carlo forgot about going slow. In fact, he forgot about everything.

He closed his fingers around her wrists and backed her against the wall, his mouth capturing her soft gasp of excitement. Her lips were soft and warm and she opened her mouth for him, tempting him inside.

He accepted the invitation, tasting her sweetness, showing her with every intimate touch of his mouth and tongue just what he wanted to do to the rest of her body.

Desire exploded inside him and he released her hands and cupped her face, sliding his hands through the silky mass of hair as he kissed her until the heat between them reached an intolerable level.

He lifted his head briefly, their foreheads touching, his expression dazed as he stared down into her eyes.

She looked as stunned as he felt, her green eyes cloudy, her soft lips bruised and damp from his kiss.

'Carlo.' She whispered his name with a reverence that made him groan and lower his mouth again.

He knew he ought to stop now, before stopping ceased to be an option, but he couldn't drag his mouth away from hers.

Her tongue teased his and he wondered how on earth he was going to keep it slow and gentle when the time came to make love to her. She drove him so wild he didn't know himself.

He felt her small hand slide under his jumper and then rest on the warm muscle of his chest, finding his heartbeat.

Muttering in Italian against her mouth, he dealt with the zip of her jeans and slid a hand inside, over the soft curve of her bottom.

'You feel incredible.' He moved his hand lower and found what he was looking for, his fingers touching her with a deliberate intimacy that brought a sob to her lips.

She moved against his hand and dragged her mouth away from his, her eyes glazed with desire and her cheeks fevered.

'Carlo, it feels so... I didn't know...'

'Shh—' He moved his hand and hugged her against him, trying to lower the temperature a notch.

He didn't succeed.

His whole body burned for this woman.

And he wasn't being honest with her.

The thought was like a shower of cold water and he released her and stepped away, raking a hand through his dark hair as he struggled with his conscience.

She leaned against the wall for support, looking at him in confusion.

Her dark hair was tangled from his touch and her cheeks were flushed. She looked like a girl who'd been thoroughly kissed and he felt desire slam through his body with a force that left him breathless.

'It's getting late. I'd better go...'

He worked on his will-power. If she asked him to stay he was in trouble.

But she didn't.

In fact, she didn't speak at all. She just stood there, supported by the wall, staring at him.

He picked up his jacket from the floor and walked back to her. He locked their hands together and bent his head to give her a gentle kiss.

'Goodnight, Zan—I'll see you tomorrow.'

And by then he would have worked out how to tell her the truth.

CHAPTER SIX

CARLO stared at the ultrasound scan and tried to forget about Zan.

She was dominating his every thought and it was starting to drive him mad.

He'd already decided that the first opportunity that he had he was going to tell her the truth and risk the consequences.

'Mr Bennett?' A young student nurse cleared her throat nervously to attract his attention. 'The labour ward has been calling. They need you up there urgently.'

Despite the fact it was Christmas Eve, the day was frantically busy and they barely saw one another as they coped with the huge workload.

Fortunately by five o'clock labour ward had calmed down and the clinic was empty.

In the nurses' locker room, Zan dragged on green tights and a figure-hugging tunic and pulled a face in the mirror. 'Are you sure this is an elf costume? I look more like Peter Pan.'

'Definitely elf,' Kim murmured as she pushed her feet into a pair of black boots. 'Next year I'm coming as something warm and furry, like a reindeer. There's something to be said for being Father Christmas. At least you can wear a thick jumper underneath. Talking of which, what's happening with that gorgeous man of yours?'

Zan blushed and tucked her dark hair under a green hat. 'He's finished on Labour Ward and he's gone to change.'

'That wasn't what I meant,' Kim said dryly, and Zan smiled.

'Nothing's happening exactly...' *Not yet anyway.* 'But we get on well. And he's such a brilliant doctor, Kim.' Her eyes shone. 'You should have seen him with Kelly. He was so calm and he just wouldn't give up on that baby. And then he managed to talk Mike round and persuade him into going to the hospital, and he'd arranged heaters and an ambulance...' She broke off, breathless, and Kim grinned.

'So you're not in love, or anything like that, then?'

Zan sucked in a breath and her eyes widened.

Love?

It had been so fast she hadn't even examined her feelings in any depth, but now she did and the result shocked her. She sat down with a thump on one of the hard chairs.

'It's only been a few days,' she croaked. 'How do I know if it's love?'

Kim shrugged. 'I don't know. Try and imagine him walking down the aisle with someone else. How do you feel?'

Zan thought about it. 'Sick?'

'That could be love or too many mince pies,' Kim said sagely. 'Do you want to punch her on the nose?'

'I think I've done enough punching in this relationship,' Zan muttered, remembering Carlo's bruised cheek. 'And I'm not kidding myself it's marriage he has in mind.'

Carlo was a red-blooded Italian male who certainly didn't need to get married to have an active sex life.

Kim shrugged. 'I wouldn't be so sure about that. He must be early thirties. All Italian men want babies at some point. They're very into the family thing. It's got to be on his agenda.'

Zan bit her lip. Did he want to get married? The thought of Carlo smiling at another woman, kissing another woman, making love to another woman, made her utterly miserable.

'OK.' She lifted her palms and gave a resigned smile. 'To answer your original question—I'd definitely want to punch her on the nose. Hard.'

Kim grinned. 'I knew it. You're in love.'

'I think I might be.' Zan's expression was gloomy. 'Bad news, huh?'

'Why bad news?' Kim straightened her costume and reached for her coat. 'He seems pretty keen on you, too.'

'Bed keen,' Zan said wistfully. 'Not marriage keen.'

'You don't know that.'

'I've only known him for four days,' Zan pointed out, and Kim shrugged.

'Well, it's been long enough for you.'

Zan thought about everything Carlo had done since she'd met him. Waded in and rescued her from being mugged, made her laugh, intervened in a difficult delivery, kissed her breathless and saved the life of a baby. She'd learned a lot about him in four days.

'He'd be a brilliant father. Oh, help!' Zan sighed. 'What's happened to me? I used to be cautious and rational. Now I want to have his babies.'

'Love is never rational,' Kim said dryly. 'When are you seeing him again?'

'Tonight.' Zan blushed slightly. 'He's staying the night so that we can open our presents together tomorrow morning. He's on call tomorrow.'

'So tonight's the night.' Kim looked at her curiously. 'Spending Christmas together sounds pretty romantic to me.'

'Well, his family is all in Italy and I can't get home so it seemed like a good idea.' Zan shrugged dismissively and Kim laughed.

'Stop making it sound like a business arrangement. You're not fooling me. What have you got planned?'

Nothing she could share with her friend.

Fortunately, before she could answer there was a knock on the door and one of the other elves stuck her head round, her eyes twinkling with fun.

'Message from Father Christmas—the reindeer are playing up and he needs some elves desperately. He's waiting for us by the main entrance.'

'Reindeer?' Kim and Zan exchanged baffled looks and made their way to the hospital entrance.

Zan pushed open the revolving doors and then stopped with a gasp of amazement.

Immediately in front of the hospital was a sleigh straight out of a fairy-tale, decorated with delicate silver chains and tiny lights and pulled by six brown reindeer with knobbly antlers and velvety noses, their breath producing clouds of steam in the frosty air.

Carlo sat holding the reins, a huge sack bulging on the seat behind him.

He was dressed as Father Christmas, most of his face concealed under a ridiculous white beard. 'Hurry up, elves. I'm never going to get down all the chimneys at this rate.'

Zan gave a laugh of delight and jumped into the sleigh next to him. 'I can't believe you found a sleigh. Did you arrange this?'

'What use is Santa without his reindeer?' His face was barely visible under the white beard that he was wearing. Then he smiled at her and bent his head for a kiss.

A laughing Kim jumped up next to them. 'Hey, this is a family show!'

They broke apart reluctantly and Carlo ran a gentle finger down Zan's flushed cheek.

'What exactly are an elf's duties?' His voice was husky with passion and Zan smiled.

'We're here to service your every need, Father Christmas.'

'Glad to hear it.' He gave her a sexy wink.

The other nurse jumped onto the sleigh and for the first time Zan noticed a girl standing next to the reindeer, holding their reins.

Once everyone was settled on the sleigh, the girl led the first pair of reindeer forward and the others followed, pulling the sleigh down the path and onto the lawn behind the children's ward.

Despite the cold and the snow, the doors had been flung open and excited children gathered in the doorway, their faces pink with delight. Those who were confined to bed had been pushed as close as possible to the window so that everyone could have a look.

Carlo said something to the girl who was helping him and she leaned forward and untied one of the reindeer, leading him carefully towards the children.

Carlo followed, leaping down from the sleigh and grabbing the bag of presents.

'Ho, ho, ho, children,' he bellowed, and Zan burst into a fit of giggles. He was the most convincing Father Christmas she'd ever seen.

He walked onto the ward and the children were soon clambering all over him, hugging him and trying to tell him what they wanted for Christmas.

Carlo listened intently and nodded and then indicated to the elves that they should give out presents.

Kim, Zan and the other nurse dipped into the enormous sack and pulled out boxes wrapped in blue and pink, passing them into eager little hands.

Several of the children were stroking the reindeer, totally enraptured by the soft covering on its antlers. It was totally docile, standing quietly while they swarmed all around it.

'I have to confess that I never knew reindeer were so small,' Kim muttered as she delved into the sack for another present.

'Does size matter in a reindeer?' Carlo's eyes twinkled suggestively and Zan laughed.

She couldn't believe he'd arranged real reindeer. When she'd asked him to be Father Christmas she'd never thought for a moment that he'd enter into the spirit of things to quite this extent.

But the children were loving every minute of it.

And as they sat on the floor, ripping open their presents, the hospital choir arrived at the entrance of the ward and started to sing carols.

The moment was so magical that Zan felt her eyes grow hot.

'I feel really Christmassy,' Kim said happily, and then she glanced across at Carlo and lowered her voice. 'He's fantastic, Zan. After tonight, I'd have his babies, too.'

Zan watched as Carlo hugged a little girl who had her leg in plaster, his dark eyes warm and kind as he listened to her breathless requests for presents.

Kim was right. He was fantastic.

And then he looked up and caught her looking at him. The benign, fatherly look in his eyes vanished, to be replaced by a look of such sexual intensity that her insides burned with excitement.

She could hardly breathe for wanting him, and she wondered how she was going to show him that she didn't want him to slow the pace any more.

It was obviously going to be up to her to take the initiative.

Finally the reindeer were loaded back into their trailer and the children were settled into bed.

'Not that I expect them to sleep much,' the ward sister admitted with a sigh as she tried to calm the excited children.

Zan moved closer to Carlo. 'How's Kelly's baby doing?'

'I've been too busy to go up and check.' He looked at her quizzically. 'Shall we go up now?'

'Dressed like this?' Zan glanced down at herself doubtfully and he laughed.

'Why not? It's Christmas Eve after all.'

So they took the lift to the labour ward and walked through to SCBU. The ward was warm and festive and the staff greeted them with amusement as they strolled onto the ward in their costumes.

'How's baby Turner?' Carlo walked over to the incubator and gazed down at the baby lying attached to tubes and monitors.

'Actually, he's doing pretty well.' The doctor looking after the baby glanced at the machines with a frown and twiddled a knob. 'They're scanning him later because they're worried about the risk of intraventricular haemorrhage.'

'Oh.' Zan looked shocked. 'Why are they worried about that?'

'It's a fairly routine procedure in premature babies,' Carlo assured her, picking up the chart and scanning it. 'Brain haemorrhage can occur in up to forty per cent of babies who weigh under 1500 grammes. How's everything else?'

The doctor adjusted her glasses. 'His blood gases deteriorated so we had to ventilate him overnight but he's stabilised now.'

She and Carlo proceeded to have a detailed conversation about the baby's progress and then Zan looked up and saw Kelly and Mike hovering in the doorway, looking out of place and uncomfortable.

'Hi.' Zan moved towards them, waving an apologetic hand over her costume. 'Sorry about the way we look—

we dressed up for the children's ward earlier and we
haven't had time to change. How are you?'

'We're fine.' Kelly looked pale and thin and she was
gazing longingly at the baby. 'He's being fed through a
tube and I so wanted to breast-feed.'

'You can still breast-feed him,' Zan assured her, taking
her arm and walking with her towards the incubator.
Machines beeped and the lights sent a glow over the dark
ward. 'Have you talked to the nurses about it?'

Kelly shook her head. 'They're so busy.'

'Not too busy to help you breast-feed,' Zan said firmly.
'What you need to do is express milk to begin with and
they can give that down his tube.'

The doctor looking after the baby glanced up and
smiled. 'In fact, that would be brilliant. He's actually not
tolerating our formula milk very well. I think it's a bit too
rich for his little tummy. Any time you want to give us
some breast milk, please, feel free.'

Kelly glanced nervously at Zan, who smiled reassuringly.

'How about now?' She sensed that Kelly was out of her
depth on this ward full of strangers. 'I could help you.
They've got a special room here where you can sit quietly.
Providing the staff don't mind me butting in, I can show
you the ropes.'

Carlo lifted an eyebrow. 'There's no end to what an elf
can do.'

Zan glanced down at herself and pulled a face. 'I'd forgotten I'm an elf.'

'I'll lend you a white coat if you'll stay and help,' one
of the nurses said dryly as she walked past and heard the
exchange.

Zan looked at Carlo. 'Is it OK?'

'Of course.' He smiled easily, as relaxed as ever. 'Give
me a shout when you're ready to go.'

He made no secret of their relationship and Zan blushed slightly.

'OK, Kelly, come with me and I'll introduce you to Daisy.'

They left Carlo talking quietly to Mike and walked down the corridor and into a small but comfortable room. Kelly hovered on the threshold.

'Who's Daisy?'

Zan laughed and waved a hand towards the machine on the table. 'Meet Daisy the cow. So called because of her role in milk production. Let me show you what to do.' She picked out various items of equipment and ripped open the packets. 'These are sterile and you need a fresh one of these every time.'

She showed Kelly what to connect where and then helped her get the pressure right on the machine.

A few drops of milk-like fluid trickled into the bottle and Kelly looked at Zan anxiously. 'It isn't very much.'

Zan sat down next to her. 'It takes a few days for your milk to come in properly. This is what we call colostrum. It's not high volume but it's very high in calories and full of antibodies.' Zan hesitated. 'You've been anaemic, Kelly, and you're pretty underweight. It's possible that you won't be able to produce enough milk to feed him completely on your own. We might need to top her up.'

Kelly's eyes filled but she nodded. 'I see.'

'It's important that you eat a good diet from now on— plenty of protein,' Zan told her, 'and keep expressing because that will stimulate your milk supply.'

Kelly looked at her. 'And will he ever be able to feed from me?'

'I'm sure he will.' Zan was quick to reassure her. 'As soon as he's a bit stronger, we'll start putting him to the breast to get him used to the idea.'

'What if he doesn't get used to the idea?'

'He will.' Zan gave her a warm smile. 'You're going to be a great mum, Kelly. How are you feeling in yourself?'

'Tired,' Kelly admitted, and Zan made a mental note to mention it to Carlo. She still needed to have her blood checked for anaemia.

'How's Mike coping?'

Kelly pulled a face. 'Pretty well, really, considering how much he hates hospitals. It brings back horrible memories for him.'

They walked back onto SCBU to find Carlo still in conversation with Mike and the doctor.

He smiled at Kelly. 'Has this little boy got a name yet?'

Kelly nodded and looked at Mike. 'Eddie,' she said softly. 'We're calling him Eddie after Mike's brother.'

There was a silence and Carlo cleared his throat. 'Good name,' he said gruffly, and Mike looked at him and rubbed a hand across the back of his neck.

'I don't know how to say this, Doc,' he mumbled, and Carlo put a hand on his shoulder, his dark eyes warm with understanding.

'There's nothing to say,' he said quietly. 'You had a difficult choice to make, but you did the right thing. You were brave.'

Mike shook his head. 'It was you who did the right thing and don't think I don't know that,' he said hoarsely. He grabbed Carlo's arm. 'You need anything—*anything at all*—you come to me.'

Carlo was visibly moved and Zan leaned forward to give Kelly a hug.

'Merry Christmas,' she said softly, looking at Eddie Turner and deciding that miracles did happen after all.

It was much later when they walked towards Zan's flat, both still dressed in costume.

'That was fun,' Carlo said, a laugh in his voice as he

reached up to rub his dark jaw. 'Apart from the beard. The beard made me itch.'

'You were brilliant.' Zan glanced over her shoulder, still nervous that someone might be following her. 'Where did you find the reindeer?'

'They came down from Scotland,' he told her, following her gaze and looking at her quizzically. 'Why do you keep looking over your shoulder?'

'Because I'm paranoid about being followed,' she confessed, moving a little closer to him. 'I thought I saw a man watching me again this morning.'

Carlo glanced at her. 'The same man from the restaurant?'

'No.' Zan shook her head. 'Someone different. Well, actually, there were two of them. I'm sure it was my imagination. I'm seeing men on every corner.'

Either way, she didn't really care at the moment. No one was going to hurt her while she was with Carlo. No one in their right mind would attack someone of his build.

They arrived back at her flat and Zan flicked on the Christmas-tree lights and lit a few candles.

She needed subtle lighting for what she had in mind.

'I put some champagne in the fridge earlier,' she murmured, moving through to the kitchen and fetching two glasses.

By the time she moved back to the sitting room Carlo had removed his hat and was wearing a snug pair of jeans and a thick jumper.

Zan's eyes twinkled. 'So this is what Father Christmas does in his spare time.'

'Consorts with elves, you mean?' He moved towards her and took the bottle, popping the cork and catching the bubbling liquid in the glasses that she held out. 'You're shivering.'

'Yes, well, elves are obviously tougher than me,' she

admitted, a plan forming in her mind. 'This outfit is freezing. I'm just going to take a shower and change into something warmer.'

Carlo tensed slightly. 'OK.'

She walked through to her bedroom, stripped off the elf costume and showered quickly.

Her heart banging against her chest, she opened a drawer and removed a bag. Did she dare?

Taking a deep breath, Zan gave a womanly smile and started to dress.

Carlo glanced towards the bedroom as he dialled, hoping that she was going to take some time.

He'd managed not to react when she'd announced that someone was still following her, but a nasty suspicion was growing in his mind.

'Matt?' He spoke in Italian, talking in a low voice as he briefly outlined the situation to the chief of security.

'I'm staying here tonight.' Carlo kept his eye on the bedroom door as he talked. 'I'm on call from eight o'clock tomorrow morning, so I could get called into the hospital then, but if I do I'll find some way of taking her with me. I don't want her left alone.'

Having agreed a plan with Matt, he ended the conversation as quickly as possible, flicking the phone shut and slipping it back into his pocket.

If there was going to be trouble, at least they were prepared.

The bedroom door opened and as he glanced up, all thoughts of danger vanished from his mind.

In fact, all rational thought vanished from his mind.

Zan was standing in the doorway looking like something straight out of a bad boy's dreams.

She was wearing skimpy briefs, sheer stockings that

made her long legs shimmer temptingly and the highest heels he'd ever seen.

Struggling to breathe, he dragged his eyes upwards, past the smooth curve of her waist and the swell of her breasts to the blatant invitation in her green eyes.

'Zan.' His voice was a tortured croak and she smiled as she walked towards him, her legs endless as she closed the gap between them.

'The other night I told you that we were going too fast.' She sounded breathy and feminine and decidedly nervous. 'I know you've been holding back, but you don't need to any more. I didn't know how to tell you…'

The draw of her smooth, creamy skin was too much, and he slid a hand around her waist, feeling the silky warmth of her skin under his fingers.

'I think I get the message.'

She trembled slightly under his touch but her gaze didn't falter. 'I want you, Carlo—if you still want me, that is.'

What a question.

Carlo almost groaned aloud. Of course he wanted her, but he needed to talk to her first. *He needed to tell her who he was.*

'Zan, I—'

He saw the uncertainty flicker in her eyes. 'Have you changed your mind?'

Zan pressed closer and his senses were swamped by her. That special scent that drove him wild, the touch of her warm skin, the feel of her breath against his cheek.

'I haven't changed my mind, but—'

'Good.' She slid her small hands under his jumper and he shuddered as he felt her fingers slide over his skin.

Part of him jerked back to reality. *He had to tell her who he was.*

'Zan, I just…'

'What?' Her voice was low and husky and she stood on tiptoe and licked at his lips in a provocative gesture that made every male hormone in his body work overtime.

He tried to capture her mouth, but she moved away with a tantalising smile that made him groan with frustration. She continued to tease him, pressing light, fluttery kisses against his mouth and cheek but dodging him when he tried to deepen the connection.

Then she tugged lightly at his jumper and he yanked it over his head and dropped it on the floor, aware that his erection was blatantly evident through the fabric of his jeans.

Her lips parted and her breathing shallow, Zan ran a finger through the dark hair on his chest, following the line downwards to where it vanished into the waistband of his jeans. She lifted her eyes to his, her gaze hot and inviting as her fingers dealt with the fastening and then the zip.

Still holding his gaze, she touched him intimately and he saw a hint of uncertainty in her eyes.

And he decided that it was time he took over.

He dispensed with his jeans and scooped her up into his arms, carrying her though to the bedroom and kicking the door closed behind them.

Her silky dark hair brushed his cheek and he lowered his head and kissed her hungrily before laying her on the bed and coming down on top of her.

She stroked a hand over the muscles of his shoulders and the trust in her eyes made something twist inside him.

He knew that they ought to be talking, not making love, but the moment for talking was long past.

All he could do now was make sure that her first time was the best time she'd ever have.

The talking would have to come later.

*   *   *

Zan lay trembling on the bed, both hands holding onto Carlo as he kissed her.

She loved the feel of solid muscle under her fingers, loved his combination of strength and gentleness.

The truth was, she loved *him*.

He lifted his head, his breathing ragged as he looked down at her, his dark eyes unbelievably sexy. Then he murmured something in Italian and the tone of his voice made her heart thump against her chest.

'You're doing it again,' she pointed out huskily. 'You're talking in Italian and I don't understand a word.'

His smile was intimate. 'I said that you are very, very beautiful, *cara mia*.'

His hand moved slowly but deliberately down her body and suddenly she found it hard to breathe. He lowered his head and kissed her slowly and the excitement he roused was so intense that it frightened her.

She pulled away slightly, stunned by how out of control she felt.

Carlo's eyes searched hers and then he gave a very male smile that showed that he understood. 'I know…'

He kissed her again, this time teasing her tongue into an erotic dance with his, arousing feelings so powerful that she pressed against him in an unspoken demand for more.

Without lifting his head, he moved his hand lower and curved it over her breast, the rough pad of his thumb teasing her hard nipple.

Sensation stabbed low in her abdomen and she gasped against his mouth and instinctively parted her legs.

He lifted his head and stroked her dark hair away from her face with a hand that wasn't quite steady.

'You are incredibly responsive, *tesoro*, and you have a disastrous effect on my self-control.' His eyes smiled into hers and he kept their gazes locked together as his hand moved lower.

Zan felt his hand on the soft skin of her thigh and then

his fingers slid inside her flimsy panties, his eyes never leaving hers as he found what he was looking for.

Her fingers tightened on the muscles of his shoulders and she tensed slightly.

'Don't be shy with me.' He murmured the words against her mouth, kissing her gently as he removed her panties. Reassuring her as his skilled fingers worked their magic. Excitement exploded inside her and she slid her hands over his skin, touching his warmth and maleness, moving her hips in an instinctive quest for satisfaction.

Carlo slid down her body, using his mouth in an exploration so thorough and intimate that by the time he finally slid back up and settled himself on top of her she was a seething, uncontrollable mass of sensation.

Desperate to know him as he knew her, she reached down to touch him, but he caught her hand and shook his head.

'No way, *tesoro*, I'm too close.'

'But—'

'There'll be time for that later.'

She felt his weight on top of her, his strength as he parted her thighs, and suddenly a flash of trepidation penetrated her consciousness.

Totally attuned to every response her body made, he slowed the pace, his dark eyes suddenly gentle as he looked down at her.

'Relax, *cara mia*. You can still change your mind.'

She didn't want to change her mind.

She wanted him to make love to her—now!

'I don't want to,' she said urgently, pulling him towards her. 'Please…'

He stared down at her, his breathing unsteady, and she could see the conflict in his dark eyes.

'If you stop now, I'll black your other eye,' she joked, her voice unsteady as she slid a hand over his smooth back.

She tugged his head down to hers and kissed him, coaxing his tongue into a game with hers.

But it was clear that he wasn't going to be rushed. His kiss was slow and leisurely, and he trailed a finger down her body, exploring her with an expert touch that drove her to fever pitch.

Finally, when she was writhing and gasping underneath him, when every part of her body ached for him, he lifted his head and looked down at her.

His gaze hot, he shifted his position slightly and entered her slowly, holding back with a visible effort, checking that she was all right.

She was more than all right.

She was in heaven.

Feeling his pulsing strength inside her, she wrapped her legs around him, her eyes locked with the heat of his as she raised her hips to meet him.

With a low groan Carlo pushed deep, driving into the heart of her, setting their bodies on fire with each skilful thrust.

Zan gasped as excitement consumed her, clutching at his hard shoulders with her fingers, feeling the strength of his body against hers.

He shifted his position slightly, his gaze locking with hers as he moved, his eyes fierce with need.

He was no longer gentle but Zan didn't even notice.

Their love-making had a wild, primitive edge to it, and she trembled beneath him as he moved inside her, deeper, harder, surrounding and filling her with his strength.

It was the most intense and intimate experience of her life.

Her climax hit without warning and she felt him shudder above her as he drove them both to a peak of excitement that consumed them both in its explosive intensity.

She clung to him, breathless and stunned, her eyes locked with his as she struggled to come back to earth.

He stroked her damp hair away from her face with a gentle hand and bent his head to kiss her again. Then he rolled over, taking her with him.

She held him tightly, relieved that he didn't seem to want to lose the physical contact.

A soft smile of satisfaction touched her lips.

She might have missed this.

If she'd been sensible and cautious she never would have invited him back to her flat on that first night, and then she never would have known what love could feel like.

He held her tightly, one arm clamping her against him, one leg slung over hers. Then he moved slightly so that he could look at her. He looked very sexy and very, very male.

'Are you OK?'

His voice was deep and accented and she gave him a shy smile.

'Are you kidding? If I'd known it was that good I would have done it years ago.'

He glowered at her and his grip tightened possessively. 'Don't say that. Ever.' His tone was raw. 'You're mine and no one else's.'

She chuckled and her eyes teased him. 'I love it when you're macho.'

He grinned and rolled her onto her back. 'I'll show you macho.'

His voice was a sexy rumble and she sighed against his mouth as he kissed her thoroughly, stoking the fire again.

'I never knew that Father Christmas had so many talents.' She lifted a hand to touch his dark jaw, loving his rough masculinity. 'I love you, Carlo.'

He stilled above her and his dark eyes narrowed slightly, revealing nothing of his thoughts.

Zan felt her cheeks warm.

She shouldn't have said anything.

Embarrassed by her declaration, and by the lengthening silence, she tried to roll away from him but his hold tightened and he used his weight to keep her still while he slid a hand into her hair, forcing her to look at him.

'I love you too.' His voice was hoarse. 'I want you to remember that, Zan. Whatever happens, I want you to remember that.'

His thumb moved gently over her cheek and she stared into his eyes, wondering what he'd meant by that remark.

Why would she need to remember that he loved her?

Something jarred inside her brain, but before she could explore the source of her unease he lowered his head and kissed her again, making her head spin and sending all rational thought from her head.

CHAPTER SEVEN

CARLO watched Zan as she slept and wondered how he'd got himself into this situation.

He'd just made love to a woman who didn't know who he was.

Shaken by the depth of his feelings, he held onto her tightly, as if keeping her close physically could prevent anything driving them apart.

He'd made love before but he realised now that it had always been a purely physical act. With Zan it had been totally different. She'd seduced his emotions as well as his body.

And when she woke up he was going to tell her the truth.

Zan smelt coffee and opened her eyes.

'Merry Christmas.' Carlo placed a tray by the bed and bent to kiss her. 'He's been.'

She sat up and rubbed her eyes, still drugged from sleep. 'Who's been?'

'Father Christmas, of course.'

Without giving her a chance to protest, he dropped an elegantly wrapped parcel into her lap and she woke up rapidly.

Her eyes widened. 'For me?'

He nodded. 'Open it.'

She tugged at the ribbon, ripped the paper and then gasped as she saw the oyster silk wrap and pyjamas.

'Oh—they're beautiful.'

She fingered them gingerly, almost afraid to touch the delicate fabric.

'Put them on.' His eyes burned into hers. 'If you don't get dressed now, I won't be able to undress you later.'

She blushed at the reminder that she was still naked, and slipped her arms into the pyjama top, loving the way the silk slithered over her skin.

'They're gorgeous.' She gazed down at herself and then up at him. 'I've never worn anything so beautiful.'

'Good.'

He smiled with satisfaction and waited for her to finish dressing. 'Now come with me.'

Still fingering the pyjamas with awe, she followed him through to the living room and gave a smile of delight when she saw the stocking stuffed full of presents lying under the tree.

'More?'

He bent his head and kissed her gently. 'Much, much more.'

She stood on tiptoe and wrapped her arms around his neck, loving the feel of his rough jaw against her skin.

'What did I do to deserve you?'

Something flickered across his face, but it was gone in an instant and he waved a hand at the bulging stocking.

'Get started. I'll fetch the coffee.'

Zan knelt down on the cushions and reached for the stocking, squeezing it as she had as a child.

'Very lumpy and bumpy.' She laughed. 'This used to be my favourite game as a child. Guessing the present. I used to break half of them before Christmas Day because I'd poked them so much.'

He sprawled alongside her and handed her a coffee. 'Drink this. It will wake you up.'

'I'm awake.' She was tugging the first present out of the stocking and ripping at the paper. 'Oh!' She picked up the pretty doll and smiled at him. 'You certainly pay attention, I'll give you that.'

'You said you'd never had one.'

'I know.' She stroked the doll's hair wistfully. 'She's beautiful.'

She worked her way down the stocking, touched by the thought that he'd put into each present. There was a book, a beautiful pen, a soft cashmere jumper in a shade of green that she knew would suit her and beautiful, feminine underwear.

'You bought me so much.' She glanced at him, embarrassed, knowing that she'd only bought him a few things and hadn't spent nearly so much.

'Put your hand in the bottom of the stocking,' he suggested, leaning forward to see what she was doing. 'There should be one more parcel.'

Zan did as she was told and withdrew a small, flat box wrapped in silver paper and bows.

'Gosh, this is elaborate.' She undid the bow, removed the paper and flipped open the box, and her face broke into a smile. 'My diamonds!'

Lying in the box were a pair of the prettiest earrings she'd ever seen.

'Do you like them?' He sounded strangely uncertain and she leaned forward to kiss him.

'I love them. They're perfect.' She lifted them out of the box and held them up to the light, watching as they twinkled and shone. 'They're *huge*! Imagine if they were real.'

There was a long silence and Carlo cleared his throat, sounding distinctly uncomfortable.

'Zan, listen—'

Suddenly aware that she might have sounded rude, Zan interrupted him.

'They're gorgeous, Carlo, and I'd hate to have real

ones,' she assured him hastily. 'I'd be terrified to wear them. Now it's my turn.' She moved over to the Christmas tree and rummaged underneath for his presents.

'This is my main present to you.' She handed him a small box, hugely pleased with herself.

The man in the shop had assured her that it was the perfect present for an Italian male. Or any male, for that matter.

Carlo ripped off the paper and stared down at the toy car in his hand.

'It's a Ferrari,' Zan said breathlessly. 'Apparently it's called an Enzo Ferrari and there aren't very many and they cost almost half a million pounds. So I thought I'd get you one for Christmas.'

Carlo was very still, staring down at the car with a strange expression on his face.

Zan's smile faded and she looked at him anxiously. 'Do you hate it? Have you already got one?'

Carlo seemed to shake himself. 'No. Not like this.'

'Good.' He seemed totally distracted and Zan looked at him in confusion. 'When I win the Lottery I'll buy you the real one.'

His eyes met hers.

'Zan, there's something I have to tell you.' His voice sounded strange and his expression was deadly serious. He put the car on the floor and reached for her hand. 'I should have told you before, but I—'

The shrill tone of his mobile phone interrupted them and he said something in Italian that she was sure wasn't polite.

'We'll talk in a moment.' He flipped open the phone. 'Carlo Bennett.' He listened, frowning slightly as the person on the other end spoke briefly. 'OK—I'll come in. Yes, she's coming, too.'

He closed the phone, his expression grim. 'Helen Hughes has gone into labour.'

'Well, what's the problem with that? Oh, no.' Zan clamped a hand over her mouth and started to giggle. 'I'd forgotten about her mother staying. She won't even have had time to put the turkey in the oven yet. Why are you looking so tense?'

Carlo hesitated. 'Because I wanted to talk to you.'

'You can talk to me while we get dressed.' Zan scrambled to her feet and dashed into the bedroom. 'What stage is she at?'

'Her waters have just broken and she's been having regular contractions for the past two hours so they've told her to come straight to Labour Ward. They wanted to let me know and I said I'll go in and check on her. I know you're not officially working until lunchtime but I thought you'd like to do the same as you're her named midwife.'

'Of course I'll come with you.' Zan dragged a uniform out of the wardrobe. 'Try keeping me away! Would you believe, I've never delivered twins? I'm really excited. This is the best Christmas ever!'

Carlo looked oddly tense as he pulled on a pair of tailored trousers and dug a roll-neck jumper out of his bag.

She reached for her coat and glanced across at him. 'What did you want to talk to me about?'

He hesitated briefly and then shrugged. 'It can wait.'

She smiled. 'We can talk tonight, after we've delivered these twins.'

Whatever it was couldn't be that important.

The two men in the car watched them leave.

'I'll say this for Santini—he's got taste,' one of the men muttered. 'That girl is gorgeous.'

His friend frowned at him. 'You shouldn't be looking at the girl. You should be looking for the bodyguard.'

'Parini?'

'He's the best there is. I'm not going near that apartment until I know he's out of the way. I value my life.'

They sat in silence for several minutes and then the larger of the two men gave a sigh of satisfaction.

'There he goes. He's not letting Santini out of his sight.'

'Which means that he's not watching the apartment. Now what?'

His friend gave a nasty smile. 'We go upstairs and leave Carlo Santini a message.'

Helen Hughes was waiting for them on the labour ward.

'How did you know?' She glared at Carlo and then screwed up her face as another contraction hit her. It was half a minute before she could finish the conversation. 'You said that I wasn't going to cook Christmas dinner. How did you know?'

'Experience. And instinct.' Carlo gave her a sympathetic smile. 'Tell me what happened.'

'I had a lousy night. Backache, leg-ache, headache— you name it, it ached. Then I got up to make a cup of tea and my waters broke so I started Christmas morning by cleaning the floor. I've been getting regular contractions ever since.'

Carlo nodded. 'OK. This is what we're going to do. I'm going to examine you to check what's happening and then, providing your cervix has dilated sufficiently, I'm going to put a scalp electrode on the first baby's head to help us monitor his heart-rate.'

Helen looked worried. 'What about the other twin?'

'We'll monitor that one externally,' Zan assured her, helping her onto the bed while Carlo washed his hands and pulled on a pair of gloves.

She opened the pack for him and got everything ready.

'You're three centimetres dilated, Helen,' he said eventually, reaching to pick up the electrode. 'I'm just going to attach this to his scalp.'

His fingers moved swiftly and skilfully and he attached the electrode with the minimum of fuss. Then he connected it to the machine.

Helen looked at it doubtfully. 'What on earth does that thing measure?'

Carlo ripped off his gloves and tossed them into the bin. 'It allows us to watch the baby's heart and how it responds during each contraction. Zan will put an external monitor on the other twin now, so that we can measure his heartbeat, too.'

Zan strapped the ultrasound transducer to Helen's abdomen and checked that she had a heart trace.

'That seems fine.' She glanced up at Carlo. 'Do you want to get a line in?'

She knew that it was important to have intravenous access in twin delivery because of the risk of complications.

'Definitely.'

He explained what they were doing to Helen and then waited until another contraction had passed before he found a vein and inserted a venflon.

'Are the babies in the right position?' Helen looked worried, but Carlo gave her a reassuring smile.

'The first baby is fine, and we don't worry about the second one until the first is safely born. Once he has room to move he might change position,' Carlo explained. 'After delivery of the first twin we will scan you to check on how the second one is lying.'

'You always call the baby *him*,' Helen pointed out tartly, and Carlo gave a sheepish grin.

'Because all Italian men are chauvinists. We always call babies *him* until proved otherwise.'

'So what happens if it's a girl?' Helen teased. 'Do you refuse to deliver it?'

'Of course not.' Carlo gave her a wink. 'I love girls.'

'I can imagine.' Helen's tone was dry and Zan changed the subject. She didn't want to think about the fact that Carlo loved girls.

'What's happening at home, Helen?' Zan handed her a drink of water and waited while she took a few sips. 'Is your husband coming in?'

Helen handed the cup back and tried to make herself more comfortable. 'Later. The children were ripping open their stockings when my waters broke, so we thought we'd try and give them as normal a Christmas as possible.' She gave a short laugh. 'I even managed to get the turkey into the oven between contractions and I did all the veg last night.'

'Sounds incredibly relaxing.' Carlo glanced up from the notes, his tone dry. 'No wonder you went into labour.'

'Well, Christmas is not the ideal time to have a baby,' Helen agreed, biting her lip and sucking in her breath as another contraction hit her. 'Ouch—this is really starting to hurt.'

'When we talked about pain relief in antenatal classes, you wanted to try and stick to gas and air,' Zan said quietly, 'but you know that you can change your mind, don't you?'

Helen breathed carefully. 'I don't know what to do any more,' she confessed. 'I read somewhere that if I have an epidural it means you can operate in an emergency.'

'I don't foresee an emergency,' Carlo said calmly. 'You do what's right for you. If we need to intervene at any stage then we'll tell you.'

Helen gave him a grateful smile. 'In that case, I'll stick to gas and air for now and see how it goes.' She looked at Zan. 'Will you be with me the whole time? It helps just to have people I trust around me.'

'I promise I'll be with you all the way,' Zan said quietly, giving her hand a squeeze.

Helen bit her lip. 'I've ruined your Christmas,' she muttered, and Zan grinned.

Ruined her Christmas?

She thought back to the night before and everything that had happened between her and Carlo.

'Are you kidding? I'm having the best Christmas I can ever remember, and delivering twins will be the highlight.' Her green eyes sparkled and she glanced up to find Carlo watching her with a heat in his eyes that made her draw breath.

He was *so* sexy.

And he loved her.

She was so happy she could barely keep it to herself.

'The labour ward staff were telling me that you weren't even supposed to be working this morning,' Helen said, clearly fretting that she'd made Zan give up her Christmas.

'I'm on a late,' Zan told her, 'which means that officially I start at lunchtime, but this is fine. I had time to open my presents.'

She looked at Carlo again, remembering the pretty earrings and the doll. He'd chosen her great presents. He wasn't just a fantastic lover and a great doctor, he was thoughtful and caring as well.

She couldn't believe she'd known him for less than a week.

Satisfied that Helen was doing well, Carlo made his excuses. 'I have to go and see some other patients now, but I'll be checking up on you and I'll be here for the delivery.'

Helen watched him go with a sigh. 'Gorgeous.'

Zan spent the rest of the morning by her side, monitoring the baby's heart and the strength of the contractions, satisfied that everything was going well.

At lunchtime she examined Helen again and found that she was seven centimetres dilated.

'This is going well, Helen,' she said, dropping her gloves in the bin and helping Helen into a more comfortable position. 'Are you sure that the gas and air is enough?'

'Just as long as you keep telling me funny stories to distract me,' Helen said, sucking in a breath as another contraction started.

Zan held her hand and encouraged her. At the end of the contraction there was a tap on the door and Kim walked in, a rope of silver tinsel wrapped around her neck and reindeer antlers on her head.

Zan looked at her. 'Something's stuck in your hair.'

Kim glared. 'Oh, very funny.' She smiled at Helen. 'I'm so sorry that Zan's your midwife today. She was all we could get on Christmas Day.'

Helen laughed. 'She's great. My favourite person, as you know.'

'Well, if you need a real midwife just press the buzzer.' Kim adjusted her antlers and grinned at her friend. 'Go and grab a coffee and a mince pie from the staffroom. I'll stay on twin watch.'

Suddenly desperate for a cup of coffee, Zan did as Kim had suggested and had just poured herself a strong cup of coffee when Carlo strolled into the room.

He looked sexy and dangerous and the look in his eyes made her heart-rate take off. Last night it had been as if they were in a separate world where reality would never intrude. Seeing him now in the staff-room, looking overwhelmingly male and very, very real, she felt suddenly shy.

'This wasn't exactly how I planned to spend the morning,' he said huskily, stepping closer to her and curving a warm hand around the back of her neck.

She glanced nervously at the door. 'We can't—not here.'

He chuckled. 'I was only planning to kiss you. If Kim can get away with wearing antlers to work, then I can certainly kiss you under the mistletoe.'

With that he lowered his head and took her mouth, exploring her fully, his free hand pulling her against his hard body.

When he finally lifted his head she was flushed and breathless and desperate for more.

More of what they'd shared last night.

'Carlo—'

He put a finger on her lips, a wry smile touching his mouth. 'I know—I feel the same way. Let's hope these twins are delivered soon so that we can both go home.'

She looked into his dark eyes, wondering what he was thinking.

He'd said that he loved her but did he really mean it?

And what did the future hold?

Did they have any sort of future?

Just after lunch Helen's husband John arrived, clutching a huge box of food, including a pile of turkey sandwiches.

'I managed to cook the lunch,' John Hughes said proudly, and Helen grinned.

'Has anyone been sick yet?'

'Charming.' He smiled at Zan. 'Have you eaten? I brought you a box of goodies for the staffroom.'

Zan thanked him and left them alone for a few minutes while she took the food to the staff room.

When she arrived back Helen was having another contraction and her husband was looking anxious.

'She says she wants to push.'

'Really?' Zan washed her hands and pulled on a pair of sterile gloves. She examined Helen carefully and then gave a smile. 'You're fully dilated, Helen, and the first head is already descending nicely. Let's try and get you a bit more upright and then I need to call in the cavalry.'

Helen gave a grunt. 'Why do we need cavalry?'

'I need to call Mr Bennett and the anaesthetist and we need to have two paediatricians—one for each twin,' Zan told her as she hit the buzzer.

Kim's antlers appeared round the door. 'Do we have lift-off?'

Zan nodded. 'Can you call the team, please?'

Kim vanished and Zan grabbed a bean bag. 'Let's try putting this behind you for a moment. It might help if you have something to push against.'

Minutes later Carlo strolled into the room dressed in theatre scrubs. His shoulders looked impossibly broad and Zan struggled to keep her attention on Helen.

He examined her quickly, checked the foetal heart trace and glanced up as one of the paediatricians entered the room.

'Just one of you?' He was frowning slightly but the doctor shook her head.

'My colleague is on her way.'

The second paediatrician arrived with the anaesthetist and from then on there was an air of anticipation and excitement as they waited for Carlo to deliver the first twin.

With the minimum of fuss and bother he delivered the head and then the shoulders and finally the first twin slipped into his hands.

'A little boy, Helen,' Carlo said quietly, letting the paediatrician check the baby carefully before putting him to the breast. 'I want him to feed if he can, because it will stimulate your contractions. In the meantime, I'm going to scan you to assess the lie of the second twin.'

Zan noted the time of delivery and carefully labelled the baby 'Twin One' so that there was no confusion.

'The second twin is lying head down, Helen,' Carlo told her finally, pressing on the top of Helen's uterus. 'I'm just moving him down a bit.'

Helen stroked the first baby's downy head and looked up at her husband in wonder. 'He's so tiny.'

Zan was concentrating on the second twin with Carlo. She glanced at the machine and placed a hand on Helen's uterus.

'She's stopped contracting.'

Carlo nodded. 'We'll put up an oxytocin infusion and wait for the head to descend.'

They did that and Zan kept monitoring the contractions. 'That's better—will you rupture the membrane?'

Carlo shook his head. 'Not yet. The baby isn't distressed, so I'd rather leave nature to take its course if we can.'

Zan looked at him with a new respect. She'd come across so many obstetricians who couldn't wait to intervene and hurry everything along, but Carlo was completely relaxed and confident, happy to let the mother's body do the work if it was possible.

Helen looked at him anxiously. 'Is it taking too long?'

'Everything's fine.' Carlo put a hand on her abdomen to feel the contraction and checked the monitor. 'We're waiting for the baby's head to come down and for the waters to break. If necessary I can speed things up, but for the moment you're doing well.'

Even as he spoke the waters broke, and when Carlo examined her again he was satisfied that the second twin's head was engaged.

'You're doing really well,' he said, encouraging Helen, who was now looking exhausted. 'Push with the next contraction.'

He shot a meaningful glance at the second paediatrician who gave a brief nod of understanding.

The second twin was born in a slippery rush and lay still in Carlo's hands. Immediately the paediatrician took the baby and cleared the airways. The baby coughed and spluttered and gave a thin wail of protest.

Zan breathed a sigh of relief and gave Helen a hug. 'Congratulations,' she said hoarsely. 'A little girl. One of each.'

'Is she all right?' Helen was straining to see the second twin, but the paediatrician was taking no chances and was giving the baby a full examination.

'She's fine,' Zan assured her. 'We're just giving her a whiff of oxygen and then you can give her a cuddle.'

Carlo delivered the second placenta, checked that it was intact and glanced at Helen. 'No tears, no stitches needed. You did brilliantly.'

Zan hid a smile. One of the main reasons that Helen hadn't encountered a problem was because Carlo was so skilled. He was undoubtedly the best doctor she'd ever worked with.

He exchanged a brief smile with Zan and then had a conversation with the paediatricians while Zan made Helen more comfortable.

The first twin was feeding happily now, firmly attached to Helen's breast, his eyes wide as he sucked.

'He's so gorgeous.' Zan touched his cheek gently.

Suddenly she had a mental picture of Carlo's babies— dark-haired and dark-eyed with seductive smiles, just like their father.

She shook herself quickly.

What was the matter with her?

She'd known him for less than a week, for goodness' sake, and here she was imagining having his babies.

She'd been spending too much time with Kim.

After they'd transferred Helen to the ward Zan grabbed her coat and went in search of Carlo.

She found him by the ward desk, finishing off some notes.

'I'm off home.'

'Wait for me!' His rough command surprised her, but she settled herself in a chair next to him and waited for him to finish writing.

Finally he closed the notes and sat back with a sigh. 'Done. Let's go. If they need me again they can call.'

They walked the short distance to her flat, and Zan was still busy chatting about the twins and the excitement of the day when the lift doors opened and she caught sight of the door of her flat.

It was splintered and torn off its hinges.

'Oh, my God.' Her face lost its colour and she made a movement towards her flat, but Carlo grabbed her and pulled her backwards.

'No!'

He thrust her behind him and reached into his pocket for his mobile phone. He keyed in a number, said a few words of Italian, his eyes never leaving the open door, and then flipped the phone shut and put it back into his pocket.

'Stay behind me.'

His harsh order made her flinch and she looked at him, startled, seeing a side of him that she hadn't encountered before.

His eyes were cold and dangerous and she swallowed hard.

'I— It's probably just kids.'

But the uneasy feeling inside her was growing.

She'd never seen Carlo this tense before. Even while delivering Kelly's baby he'd been relaxed and amazingly cool.

Something was very wrong.

He walked softly to the door and looked inside, his jaw tightening as he saw the mess in her flat.

'Oh, no!' She peeped around his shoulder and gave a groan as she saw the Christmas tree lying on its side, the presents scattered around the living room. 'My tree! My things…'

Her favourite blue sofa had been torn apart and glasses had been smashed on the wooden floor.

'Who would want to do this?' Distressed by the mess, she pushed past him and dropped to her knees, tears filling her eyes as she picked up some of the presents. 'Who would want to rob someone on Christmas Day?'

It seemed so unfair that she stifled a sob, aware that Carlo was prowling around her flat, checking every room, his face dark and dangerous.

She stared at him, puzzled by his behaviour. 'What are you doing? They're not likely to still be here. It was just children.'

Zan brushed the tears away from her face and scrambled to her feet, frowning slightly as her eyes rested on the television and the stereo.

'That's odd.'

'What's odd?' Carlo's tone was clipped as he moved towards the doorway of her flat, obviously waiting for someone.

'They don't seem to have taken anything.' Zan glanced around the room and then bent down and picked up the earrings that Carlo had given her for Christmas. 'Why would anyone break in and not take anything?'

Carlo's sucked in a breath. 'Zan—'

Before he could finish what he was going to say the lift doors opened and a man stepped out.

Zan's eyes widened. It was the same man who'd been following her and who Carlo had spoken to in the restaurant.

She looked at him in confusion and then back at Carlo, who was speaking in rapid Italian.

Then she heard footsteps on the stairs and armed police swarmed into her flat.

'What the hell is going on?' She backed away, intimidated by the sight of guns and bulletproof vests. She stared at Carlo in shock and then looked at one of the policeman.

'They've broken in and trashed the place but they don't seem to have taken anything.' Her voice tailed off as she watched them comb the flat, suddenly aware that they weren't interested in her. It was like something out of the movies and a chill spread over her body.

Why were they turning up with guns?

She didn't fool herself that the police took breaking and entering that seriously.

Something else was going on.

One of the policemen was talking to Carlo, his manner respectful. 'We've had them under surveillance since they entered the country but they gave us all the slip last night. They were obviously hiding out somewhere, waiting for you to go to the hospital.'

Zan stared. Who? Who had been hiding out?

Carlo's mouth was grim. 'How did they find me?'

The policeman gave a wry smile. 'It's hard for anyone as well known as you to hide anywhere for long. Someone somewhere would have spotted you and passed on the information. We've had calls from the press, too, so I think it's safe to assume that your secret is well and truly out.'

Well known? Secret?

Why were the police treating Carlo as if he were royalty?

Zan had had enough. She stalked up to Carlo, her face pale. 'Would someone mind telling me what's happening?'

The policeman was still looking at Carlo. 'This was probably a warning. They want you to know that they've discovered your identity and that they're on to you.'

'I realise that.' Carlo let out a long breath as he turned

to Zan. 'I need to get you away from here. I never should have dragged you into this.'

'Dragged me into what?' Zan looked round at the armed police and shivered with cold. Then she looked back at Carlo, but suddenly he seemed like a stranger. Gone was the warmth and good humour that she'd come to expect from him. In its place was a tough, ruthless detachment which she found intimidating. 'What's all this about discovering your identity? Just who the hell are you?'

Her voice rose and Carlo stiffened. 'Zan, listen—let me sort this out and then we'll talk.'

'No way.' She shook her head and planted herself firmly in front of him, ignoring the police and the other man who clearly knew Carlo well. 'We talk now.'

'All right.' He ran a hand over his dark hair and let out a long breath. 'My surname isn't Bennett.'

There was a long silence while Zan digested that piece of information. *Not Bennett.* She remembered that first day when Kim had spoken to him and he hadn't reacted to his name. No wonder. He hadn't recognised it.

He'd been lying to her. Suddenly she found it difficult to breathe. *He'd been lying to her from the first evening they'd met.*

How could she have been so gullible?

It had all been too good to be true.

Her eyes were hurt and accusing. 'So, what *is* your name?'

'It's Santini,' he said quietly, and she stared at him in silence, wondering why the name was familiar.

Santini.

Suddenly her eyes widened. 'As in SMS? Santini Medical Supplies?'

SMS was a huge multinational corporation. Massive. Everyone had heard of it.

Somehow she found her voice. *'That's you?'*

A muscle worked in his dark jaw. 'It's my father,' he admitted. 'I don't get involved. I really do run a women's clinic in Milan. I left Italy to get away from some men who were threatening me. The authorities arranged for me to work under a different surname.'

She licked dry lips. 'You lied to me?'

'I tried to tell you last night.'

'But you didn't try that hard, did you?' She closed her eyes briefly, remembering just what had happened the night before. Just what she'd let him do. *Just how much she'd trusted him.*

Oh, God, how could she have been so stupid?

She'd made love to a stranger.

A stranger who had been deceiving her all the time.

'I trusted you…' Her voice was little more than a whisper as her mind ran over all the intimacies she'd allowed him. *'I trusted you.'*

Oblivious to the curious stares of the policemen, she backed away, looking at him with such pain in her eyes that he sucked in a breath.

'And you can still trust me.' His tone was urgent. 'We'll sort this out, Zan, I promise.' He reached out and grabbed her hands. 'But for the time being we just need to get you somewhere safe.'

She jerked her hands away and looked at him, her eyes glistening with tears. 'I was safe before I met you.'

He flinched visibly and she knew that he'd understood the depth of meaning behind her words.

It wasn't just the criminals who had rocked her life; it was *him*. By deceiving her.

'Why are they after you?'

Carlo was tense, rattled out of his usual cool. 'One of my patients had a stillborn baby. There was absolutely no way my staff could have prevented it. It was one of those sad cases that just happen. But the father blamed me.'

'And he's trying to *kill* you?' She stared at him, aghast. 'Don't Italian people ever communicate? Don't they have things like counselling in Italy?'

'He was past counselling,' Carlo said wearily. 'When a child dies the parents often look for someone to blame; you know that. It's normal.'

'And you just accept that?'

'No, of course not. But I can't help him if I can't find him. So far I've received nothing but threats. We were hoping that by leaving Italy we might be able to lure him out into the open.'

She gave an incredulous laugh. 'So you're saying you *wanted* him to follow you?'

Carlo dragged long fingers through his dark hair and nodded. 'Yes. He was threatening my family. We thought that if I left Italy it might be safer for everyone.'

'Except you.'

'I can take care of myself.'

'And what about me?' Her eyes were bright. 'It's *my* flat they've trashed Carlo. *Mine*.'

'I can put that right.' His jaw tightened. 'And as for you personally you've been watched every minute of the day since we met. I would never put you in danger—'

One of the policemen cleared his throat. 'We need to fingerprint this place.'

Carlo nodded and moved out into the corridor, taking Zan by the arm. 'Listen, I'm going to take you somewhere safe until this is over.'

She shook his arm off and turned to look at the man who'd been following her. 'And who's he? One of your henchmen?'

Carlo frowned at her description. 'He's my father's chief of security and he's the best there is. He's had you in his sight from the day after you met me.'

'Well, if that's supposed to make me feel better then

I'm afraid it doesn't.' Zan stared at him, her mind working overtime. 'Was he the reason you knew I went to Kelly's?'

Carlo hesitated and then nodded, and she turned to Matt, tears glistening in her eyes.

'So if you're so good, why didn't you stop them trashing my flat?'

'I wasn't watching your flat. I was watching you,' Matt said quietly, his eyes sympathetic. 'Look, I can understand why you're upset, but Carlo wasn't in a position to tell you. Try and understand. He'd only just met you—he didn't know you well enough to trust you.'

'Is that so?' She planted herself in front of Carlo, brushing away the tears that trickled down her cheek. 'You knew me well enough to go to bed with me and say that you loved me, just not well enough to be honest and tell me who you really were.'

Carlo tensed. 'Zan, listen, we—'

'I don't want to listen. I just want you to answer me something honestly.' Her voice was hoarse as she interrupted him. 'Clearly everyone knows who you are, and I suppose I should have recognised you, too. I've seen your picture often enough in those stupid glossy magazines. But I didn't. And what I want to know is why a multimillionaire would be interested in me. What were you doing, Carlo? Slumming it?' She stepped closer to him, her small fists clenched by her sides, her green eyes on fire. 'Were you finding out how the other half live? Using me as a distraction for your brief spell in exile?'

'*Dio*, it wasn't like that.' His words were heavily accented and she could tell that he was longing to break into Italian. 'It's true that it was a refreshing change, being with someone who didn't know who I was, but that had nothing to do with our relationship.'

'It had everything to do with it,' she said flatly, the anger suddenly subsiding. In its place was a numbness that slowly worked its way through her whole body. 'You could have told me who you were if you'd wanted to. But you didn't trust me enough. I was good enough to sleep with, but not good enough to confide in.'

He frowned. 'That isn't true.'

'Yes, it is. You didn't trust me, did you, Carlo?'

He hesitated a fraction too long. 'You have to understand something—'

'I understand everything. Our whole relationship has been based on a lie, hasn't it? So tell me one more thing.' She tilted her head on one side, her green eyes challenging him. 'Just how much money *have* you got, Carlo?'

He sucked in a breath. 'Enough.'

'Which, roughly translated, means that you're loaded,' she said. 'That toy Ferrari I gave you this morning—you gave it a really odd look. You've got the grown-up version at home, haven't you?'

He had the grace to look uncomfortable. 'Yes, but—'

Half a million pounds' worth of car.

'And the earrings…' A thought occurred to her and she stuck her hand in her pocket and removed them. She stared down at them, sparkling in her palm, a vivid and cruel reminder of what they'd shared only that morning. 'Oh, my God…'

How could she have been so naïve?

She studied them, speechless. Then she thrust them into his hand.

'They're real, aren't they?'

'Yes.' Carlo met her gaze head-on and she shook her head in disbelief.

'You did the Lottery with me, you helped me plan how you'd spend the money, and all the time you've got more money than you know what to do with.'

'Zan, you're not making any sense.' His tone held a hint of exasperation. 'So I've got money. Why does that mat-

ter? You're always planning how you'd spend money—
well, now you *can* spend it.'

She shook her head, her expression incredulous. 'You
just don't get it, do you? We laughed together, we shared
things, but none of it was real. You lied to me. *I don't
know who you are.*'

His jaw tightened. 'I'm the same man who made love
to you last night.'

She lifted a hand and slapped him hard across the face,
wounded by his blunt reminder.

'And I hate you for that!' Her voice rang with passion
and she glared at him. 'And I don't want your babies any
more—and if you'd married someone else I *would* have
punched her on the nose, but now she can have you!!'

With that she turned on her heel and made for the stairs,
ignoring the lift which was still standing open.

She'd wanted to have his babies?

Carlo blinked, trying to make sense of her tumbled
speech. Punched who on the nose? Who was she saying
could have him?

He was still pondering the answer as he sprinted after
her, with Matt close behind. 'Zan, wait!'

He heard her footsteps clattering on the stairs as she fled
from him and cursed fluently under his breath.

He didn't want her out there alone.

Finally they reached street level and he slammed
through the doors and stared around, looking for her.

Everything was quiet. She'd vanished.

Carlo whirled around and paced up to Matt. 'We've got
to find her,' he growled ominously. 'Before *they* do.'

CHAPTER EIGHT

'LET me get this straight.' Kim reached for a second box of tissues. 'You found out that he's a millionaire—no, sorry, a *multimillionaire*—and you slapped his face and walked away from him?'

Sitting cross-legged on the bed, Zan helped herself to a bunch of tissues and blew her nose hard. 'Basically, yes.'

'Right.' Kim gave her a look of total incomprehension. 'But you love the guy, yes?'

'Yes. No. I don't know any more.' Zan's eyes filled again and Kim gave a sigh.

'You love him. I recognise the signs. And frankly I'm missing something here. You love him, you slept with him, but now you've found out he's rich you're walking away from him.' She pulled a face. 'Sorry, but it doesn't make sense.'

'It isn't the money,' Zan sniffed. 'It's because he *lied* to me. He didn't tell me who he really was.'

Kim spread her hands. 'Well, the guy was obviously in a spot of bother.'

A spot of bother.

Zan remembered the police, the guns and the mess in her flat.

'I think he was in more than a spot.'

'Well, then, you can hardly blame him for keeping his identity a secret,' Kim reasoned. 'He had a bunch of thugs after him.'

'He should have told me.' Zan blew her nose again and settled herself more comfortably on the bed. 'I feel totally humiliated. As though I slept with a stranger.'

'Well, you did in a way. But that's OK,' Kim added hastily. 'I mean, you liked him. A lot. More than you've ever liked a man before.'

'That was when I thought he was a normal person.'

'He is a normal person.'

Zan shook her head. 'He's super-rich, Kim. Bodyguards, private planes, homes around the world. Where do I fit into all that?' She jettisoned the tissues and stood up, padding over to the mirror. 'You've seen the magazines. The guy dates models and actresses. What's he doing with me?'

She stared gloomily at her blotched reflection and Kim sighed.

'Well, when you're not howling you don't look too bad. He was having a good time. Zan, you're gorgeous. You just don't see it yourself and you never have.'

Zan shook her head. 'The truth is, he was with me because it was a refreshing change to be with someone who didn't know who he was.'

Kim shrugged. 'Well what's wrong with that? It must be pretty tough, being a multimillionaire. How can you trust anyone's motives? At least he knew you wanted to be with him for himself.'

'But what about *me*? Didn't he think about me? He should have told me.'

'Yes, well, maybe he should,' Kim conceded, 'but look on the bright side. You've got a *very* rich boyfriend. At the very least you should get some decent Christmas presents.'

Zan sniffed. 'He gave me diamond earrings.'

'Really?' Kim's eyes widened and she gave a slow smile of approval. 'Good for him.'

'I gave them back.'

Kim stared at her in disbelief. 'Are you mad?'

'No.' Zan looked at her, trying to make her understand.

'He let me believe they were fake, just like he let me believe that what we had together meant something. Once I found that the earrings were real I couldn't keep them. They were part of the deception.'

'You gave diamond earrings back because they *weren't* fake?' Kim stared at her in obvious confusion. 'You're a disgrace to women. And you're making no sense whatsoever.'

Zan struggled to explain. 'I thought I knew what they were but then they turned out to be something different. Like Carlo.'

'I wish I could say that I understand,' Kim muttered, lifting a hand and scratching her head. 'But, frankly, I don't.'

Zan took a deep breath, her expression bleak. 'I don't know who he is.'

Kim stood up and gave her a hug. 'Of course you do. The money doesn't change anything.'

'It changes *everything*,' Zan said flatly, pulling away from her and walking across the room. 'Can't you see that? He isn't the man he pretended to be. His lifestyle is totally different. He's only here for a short time and once they've caught the idiots who are threatening him he'll be back in Italy, running his exclusive clinic and jetting between his different homes. I was just a temporary distraction and I was a fool to have trusted him.'

'Whoa!' Kim held up a hand. 'You're making lots of assumptions here. Have you tried discussing this with him?'

'Only long enough for me to make a total fool of myself in front of half the police force.' Zan turned and walked back again. 'I told him I didn't want his babies, that I wouldn't punch the woman who married him on the nose and to finish it all off I've probably blacked his other eye.'

'Really?' Kim looked intrigued. 'Did the police arrest you for bodily harm?'

Zan gave a groan and lifted a hand to her aching head. 'Don't even joke about it. I was angry. He lied to me!'

'Don't worry about the punch. Men love a feisty woman,' Kim assured her, frowning as Zan turned and walked again.

'Can you stop pacing for a moment?' She glared at her in exasperation. 'You're wearing out a perfectly good carpet.'

'Pacing helps me to think.'

Kim sighed. 'OK, so what happens next?'

Zan paced again. 'I redecorate my flat and get on with my life. And next time try not to be so gullible.'

Kim looked doubtful. 'You think he'll leave it at that?'

'Of course he will.'

'I wouldn't be so sure. He's a pretty confident guy,' Kim said. 'He's going to go after what he wants.'

'But he didn't want me,' Zan said in a choked voice. 'Not really. I was just a novelty. Someone who didn't know who he was.'

But now she knew the truth.

Their whole relationship had been false.

Zan awoke on Boxing Day with a terrible headache and a hollow feeling in her stomach. Nursing a cup of coffee in Kim's sitting room, it seemed as if the Christmas decorations had somehow lost their sparkle.

Like her life.

She'd never experienced such extremes of emotion in such a short space of time. She'd gone from being ecstatically happy to utterly miserable in less time than it took to say 'mistletoe'.

Deciding that the only way forward was to just get on

with her life, she borrowed one of Kim's uniforms and went to work with her head held high.

She wasn't going to cry.

Fortunately no one but Kim knew about her relationship with Carlo, so there wouldn't be any pitying glances.

There was no clinic because it was Boxing Day, so she was sent to work on the labour ward, which was frantically busy.

'Can someone go out and look for a warm stable?' one of the midwives quipped. 'There's no more room at the hospital.'

'I feel sorry for all these babies born at Christmas,' Kim said as she fixed her antlers in place for the second day running. 'Imagine—they're facing a lifetime of joint presents. Talk about cruel.'

Despite her smile, Kim was looking tired and worried, and every now and then she gave Zan a searching look, checking that she was OK.

Zan tried to smile back, telling herself not to be so pathetic.

A week ago she hadn't even met Carlo and she'd been happy enough then. Surely it wouldn't take long to get back to normal?

But a week ago she hadn't been in love.

The sister in charge took her to one side. 'There's a patient in Room 3 who's requesting that you take care of her. She wasn't registered with us, so I suppose she must be a friend or something.'

Zan frowned. She didn't have any pregnant friends.

'Her name is Abby Santini. Ring any bells?'

Zan sucked in a breath. A relative of Carlo's? But why would she be asking for her?

'Her husband is a top paediatric cardiac surgeon,' the sister told her. 'He actually worked here for a short while and I remember him vaguely. Scarily brilliant and doesn't suffer fools—you know the type.'

My brother is a doctor.

Zan racked her brains to remember what Carlo had told her about his family and didn't come up with much.

He'd hardly told her anything, she realised dully. He'd managed to dodge most of her questions and she really knew next to nothing about him.

'I don't know them.'

The sister frowned slightly. 'Well, they asked for you by name, and they need someone good, so unless you've got a problem with it you can be their midwife.'

She had a big problem.

Spending a day with Carlo's family wasn't part of her rehabilitation. And if his brother's wife *was* in the unit then that must mean that Carlo would turn up at some point, and when that happened she didn't want to be near the place.

Reminding herself never to go off with strangers again, she walked down the corridor, tapped on the door of Room 3 and walked in, determined to persuade them to choose another midwife.

A broad-shouldered man had his arm round a very pretty young blonde woman who was gasping in pain.

Zan frowned, forgetting her problems for a moment as she hurried across to her. 'Is it bad?'

'Terrible.' The young woman could hardly speak, her eyes closed in agony.

'Breathe in through your nose, out through your mouth—slowly,' Zan instructed. 'That's better. And again…'

She helped Abby with her breathing until the contraction had ended and then moved her across to the bed.

'Slip your shoes off and pop up on there. I'll need to

examine you and then we'll have a conversation about pain relief.'

Abby caught her breath and then looked at her curiously. 'Are you Zan?'

Zan reached for the blood-pressure cuff and nodded, trying not to look at the dark-haired man hovering next to them. He was breathtakingly handsome.

And he looked like Carlo.

'I'm Abby.' The young woman gave her a friendly smile. 'We've heard lots about you—Carlo said you're the best midwife he's ever worked with. This is my husband, Nico.'

'Nice to meet you.' Zan felt a lump building in her throat and concentrated on taking her patient's blood pressure.

'That's fine.' She removed the stethoscope from her ears and sat down on the bed with a blank set of notes. 'You're not booked in with us so I don't know your medical history.'

Abby smiled. 'I'm booked at Carlo's clinic in Milan, but then he had to come here so I followed him. I've been staying in London for the past few weeks. I wanted him nearby when I delivered.'

She obviously thought that Carlo walked on water.

Zan tried to smile. 'So…' The words stuck in her throat. 'Does Carlo know you're here?'

'Of course.' It was his brother who spoke this time, his English perfect. 'He's joining us shortly.'

And at that moment the door opened and Carlo strode in, his face strained.

'*Ciao, bella.*' He embraced Abby and his brother and proceeded to conduct a conversation in rapid Italian while Zan tried not to look at him.

That one quick glance when he'd walked through the

door had been more than enough to remind her of why she'd behaved so recklessly.

He was stunningly good-looking and had an air of calm authority that transmitted itself to those around him. No wonder she'd fallen so hard. What woman wouldn't? What she needed to know was how she was going to get up again.

Finally he ended the conversation and gave Abby a reassuring smile. 'It will be fine, *angelo*. Trust me.'

Unable to stand any more, Zan gritted her teeth and left the room to fetch the CTG machine that would measure Abby's contractions and the baby's heart-rate.

Trust him.

She'd done that once and look where it had led her.

Carlo followed her out of the room and walked purposefully across to where she was standing.

She tensed, painfully conscious of his close proximity.

'Her blood pressure is fine,' she said formally. 'I haven't examined her yet, but I'm going to do that next. She seems to be having quite strong contractions so I need to talk to her about pain relief and—'

'Zan,' he interrupted her, his voice low. 'Abby can wait for one more minute. We need to talk about last night.'

Zan froze and her fingers tightened on the machine.

'No, we don't.' She took several breaths and then lifted her chin. 'Frankly, I didn't even expect you to be at work. I assumed you would have gone back to your old life. Tell me, what name are you using today? Santini or Bennett?'

He flinched visibly and muttered something under his breath. 'I asked you to trust me, Zan. I would have told you who I was. I would have explained everything if you hadn't run away.'

Easy enough to say that now.

'So, did they catch them?'

He shook his head, his dark eyes weary. 'Not yet. Which

is another thing we need to talk about. The police don't think you should return to your flat for the time being. It isn't safe. I want you to come and stay at my apartment.'

No way. It would be torture.

'I've found my own accommodation.'

'With Kim.'

Her eyes widened. 'Are you still having me followed?'

He nodded. 'And don't expect me to apologise for it. I put you in danger, the least I can do now is keep you safe. I'm just sorry it ruined your Christmas.'

She felt tears prick her eyes. Oddly enough, it wasn't the trauma of the break-in that had ruined her Christmas as much as his betrayal.

'You should have told me the truth right at the beginning.' Her voice shook with emotion. '*You* should have trusted *me*.'

'I can understand why you think that.' His voice was soft, his dark eyes holding hers, refusing to let her look away. 'But maybe if I tell you a little bit about my life you might understand why I didn't tell you straight away. And I *was* going to tell you, Zan. You have to believe that.'

She took a step backwards, unnerved by the way he made her feel.

'Women get involved with me for all sorts of reasons, none of them the usual ones.' Carlo's tone was resigned. 'Usually it's because they find my wallet attractive, sometimes it's the so-called status of being seen with me. I admit it's been a long time since I trusted a woman. Not since someone I thought I was close to sold intimate details about my family to the press for a great deal of money.'

Zan winced. 'That's awful. But you know I wouldn't do that.'

'I think it's unlikely, but you'd be amazed what people will do when they're offered money.' He sounded tired.

'The truth is that part of me is still wary, and I wanted our relationship to develop before I revealed the reality. I admit that I really, really enjoyed the fact that you didn't know who I was.'

Zan felt totally confused. 'But what we shared wasn't real.'

'It was real, Zan. For me it was even more real because you didn't know who I was.' He moved closer to her, his voice low and urgent. 'You spent time with *me*, away from the money and the crazy lifestyle. I always knew that we couldn't live in a cocoon for ever, that sooner or later I'd have to tell you, but I hoped that by then what we had together would be strong enough to withstand the realities of my life. Unfortunately they intruded sooner than I'd planned and I didn't have time to tell you the truth myself.'

She looked at him uncertainly, trying to think objectively and failing dismally. When he was this close she couldn't think at all. She was breathlessly aware of his overwhelming physical presence, his masculinity and the unexpectedly gentle look in his eyes.

But he'd fooled her before. 'Without trust there can be no relationship.'

'I do trust you, Zan.' His eyes were steady on hers. 'Because you didn't know who I was, I can be totally sure that what you felt was for me alone, not for my name or my connections. I trust you completely. Now it's up to you to decide whether you can trust me.'

Could she?

'How will I know that you're not keeping more secrets?' Zan's voice was choked and he cursed under his breath and pulled her towards him.

'Because from now on whatever I tell you will be the truth.' His fingers tightened on hers. 'The press print something different about me almost every day, just because of my name. Some of it is total fabrication, and some of it comes from people with a grudge. It doesn't matter where it comes from; the press are constantly digging for dirt. No relationship of mine has ever survived the intense scrutiny that I'm subjected to on a daily basis. I swear that from now on I won't hold anything back from you, but in return you have to be able to ignore all the things that people say about me. If you can't trust me, Zan, we don't stand a chance.'

Did he really believe that they might still have a future together?

Zan stared at him in confusion, but before she could answer the door opened and Nico walked out, looking tense. He said something to his brother in Italian and Carlo nodded.

'We need to get back to Abby.'

Suddenly aware that they'd been having an intensely personal conversation in the middle of the corridor, Zan glanced around self-consciously and started to push the machine to Abby's room.

Ten minutes earlier she'd been totally sure that she could never forgive him. But now nothing seemed clear.

Could she trust a man who hadn't been entirely honest with her, even if he'd had good reason for the deception?

She walked back to the bedside, trying to hide her feelings, but then she met Abby's searching gaze and felt her eyes fill.

Abby said something in Italian to the two men and then took Zan's hand. 'If you're going to examine me then I'd rather they went and had a coffee. I don't need an audience.'

Carlo frowned. 'I ought to examine you.'

Abby smiled calmly. 'This is my second baby, Carlo. I need you around for emergencies but so far there isn't one and Zan and I can manage fine on our own. Take Nico to find some coffee. He's a nervous wreck.'

Carlo hesitated and then caught his brother's eye and nodded briefly. 'All right. We'll be back in ten minutes.'

They left the room and Abby screwed up her face as another contraction hit her.

'Oh, help—my first delivery was nothing like this. I'm trying not to be a baby but I'm in agony.'

Zan slid an arm around Abby's shoulder and helped her with her breathing until the contraction passed.

Abby flopped back against the pillow. 'OK. We need to talk fast before the next one hits me. What's going on with you and Carlo?'

Zan flushed. 'Nothing—we're just colleagues.'

'Then why do the pair of you look so miserable? There's one thing you should know about Italian families,' Abby said gently, 'and that's that they're very close. Carlo's been talking to his brother regularly. Nico has known about you from the first. We were all getting excited that Carlo might finally have found someone he could be happy with.'

Zan bit her lip. 'He told you about me? But he's known me for less than a week.'

'And you made a real impact,' Abby said. 'I've never known him seriously smitten before. So what went wrong?'

Zan bit her lip. 'He lied to me. He told me nothing about himself and he used a false name.'

Abby sucked in a breath and put a hand on her stomach. 'Hold that thought—I've got another contraction coming.'

Zan took her hand and coached her through it, reminding her how to breathe.

The contraction passed but Abby held onto her hand. 'He had to use a false name,' she said, struggling to get her breath back. 'The press have been hounding him in Italy. After that baby was stillborn he started to receive death threats and there's been a massive security operation ever since. It's been awful for him.'

Zan gave a wan smile. 'I still think he could have trusted me.'

'Perhaps he could, but if you knew the attention that the Santini family attracts in Italy you'd understand why he didn't,' Abby said. 'It's pretty hard for them to trust anyone. Carlo really liked the fact that you didn't know who he was. For once in his life he was able to have a normal relationship with someone.'

'But it wasn't normal, was it? I didn't know who he was.'

Abby looked at her thoughtfully. 'Tell me what you love about Carlo.'

Zan sat down on the edge of the bed, not even bothering to deny her love. It was obvious. 'I love his sense of humour. I love the way he's so relaxed and confident. I love his strength, and I even love the fact that he doesn't know how to be politically correct about women.'

Abby laughed. 'All Italian men are like that. Carry on. What else do you love?'

Zan shrugged. 'I love the fact that he's such a great doctor and I love the fact that he has such a strong bond with his family.'

Abby nodded with satisfaction. 'And all those things that you love about him are still there, no matter what his name is. Having a different name doesn't change the person.'

Which was basically what Carlo had said.

'It hurts that he didn't trust me enough to tell me his name,' Zan muttered, and Abby sighed.

'That's true, but he's trusting you now. You've got plenty of information which you could take to the press. 'They'd probably pay quite a lot of money for your story.'

Zan frowned. 'I wouldn't do that.'

'I know. But he's been so badly burned in the past that trust doesn't happen overnight for him.'

Zan gave a short laugh. 'And I thought *I* was the one who has problems trusting.'

'One of the reasons that the Santini family is so close is because outsiders have let them down so badly. They've learned to trust their own and no one else.'

Zan nodded. 'I'm beginning to see that.'

'You know, if you talk to him you can still sort this out.'

Zan shook her head. 'I don't know.' She swallowed back a lump in her throat. 'He needs me to trust him unconditionally and I don't know if I can do that.'

What if he hurt her again?

'But you didn't understand anything about his background until he explained who he was,' Abby pointed out. 'And now you do, so surely you can forgive him. You both love each other and that has to count for something.'

Did it? Zan wasn't sure anymore.

She stood up and washed her hands. 'I really ought to examine you. They'll be back any minute and all we've done is talk.'

'Nothing wrong with that.'

Zan looked at her curiously. 'You're not Italian, are you?'

'English.' Abby wriggled down the bed so that Zan could feel her abdomen. 'I first met Nico when I was at school with his sister, and then we met up again years later. It's a pretty complicated story.'

Zan lifted Abby's jumper and ran her hands skilfully over her bump, feeling for the baby's position. 'I'm starting to expect nothing less from the Santini family. Their whole lives are obviously very complicated. So this is your second child?'

'We have a little girl who's just two. She's called Rosa.'

'And you live in Italy?' Zan's hands kept moving and she frowned slightly as she palpated one part of the abdomen and looked at the shape of Abby's stomach.

'Well, Nico works mostly in a hospital in Milan, but he's brilliant at his work and gets invited to all sorts of places to teach.' She smiled proudly as she spoke. 'And wherever he goes, Rosa and I go with him.'

'So where's Rosa now?'

'Nico owns an apartment in Knightsbridge,' Abby said. 'She's there with our nanny. Why are you frowning?'

Zan finished her examination. 'Abby, your baby is in what we call an occipitoposterior position, which basically means that his back is lying along your back.'

'Is that why I'm in so much pain?'

Zan nodded. 'Let me just examine you internally and then we'll talk about a plan of action.'

She washed her hands and pulled on a pair of sterile gloves. 'OK, this might be a bit uncomfortable but hopefully not too much...'

She was as quick as she could be. 'You're four centimetres dilated, Abby.'

Abby gave a groan and wriggled upright again. 'Is that all? Another six centimetres to go? I'll die.' She gasped as another pain hit her and this time the gasp turned to a sob. 'This is agony. I don't think I can stand it.'

'It's because of the way the baby is lying,' Zan explained. 'I think you should seriously consider having an epidural.'

Abby pulled a face. 'Nico doesn't really want me to.'

Zan smiled sympathetically. 'That's because he doesn't know the details and because he's a doctor. They're always the worst when their wives are in labour. I'll talk to him when he comes back. I think Carlo will agree with me in the circumstances.'

At that moment the door opened and Nico strolled back into the room, deep in conversation with his brother.

Zan walked up to him and came straight to the point. 'Abby needs some pain control. The baby's OP. She's four centimetres dilated and she's starting to get distressed with each contraction. She's still got a long way to go.'

Carlo frowned. 'You're sure it's OP?'

Zan nodded. 'She's got a saucer-shaped depression just below the umbilicus, the head is high and I just examined her and the anterior fontanelle is in the anterior part of the pelvis.'

Nico tensed and looked at his brother. 'What does all that mean?'

'Let me examine her and then we'll talk.'

Carlo sat down on the edge of the bed and kissed his sister-in-law on both cheeks, his affection obvious.

'Is it bad, *angelo*?'

Abby nodded, her face white and drawn. 'I thought second births were supposed to be easier, but this is much, much worse than Rosa.'

Carlo ran a hand over the top of her abdomen, feeling the contraction as it hit, holding Abby's hand as she gasped.

Carlo talked to her quietly, encouraging and supporting her, his calm tone totally reassuring. Zan watched him, realising with a sick feeling that she loved him as much as ever.

Once the contraction had passed Carlo stood up and examined Abby, his eyes clashing with Zan's.

'You were right. She's OP.' He frowned. 'When were you last checked by a doctor?'

Abby blushed. 'A while ago.'

Nico was looking tense. 'Is someone going to tell me what's wrong?'

Finally Carlo stood up. 'Nothing's wrong. The baby is

lying in the occipitoposterior position,' he told his brother. 'We call it OP.'

'What does that mean?'

Nico wanted medical facts and Carlo gave them willingly.

'It means that labour will probably be prolonged. The head isn't flexed and doesn't fit well onto the cervix. Because of that, it doesn't stimulate effective contractions. The head has to flex and rotate into the right position so that delivery can occur normally.'

Nico's eyes narrowed and his gaze was sharp. 'And if it doesn't?'

'She may need forceps or a Caesarean section. Either way it will be easier and safer if she has an epidural in place. It will also be less distressing for her. Zan's right that she still has a long way to go.'

Nico sucked in a breath. 'I don't want someone poking her in the back.'

'I understand your concern but the anaesthetist is excellent.' Carlo put a hand on his brother's shoulder and took a deep breath. 'If I had a baby with a heart defect I would put it in your hands because you're my brother and I trust you. You have to do the same with me. You have to think about what's best for Abby.'

Nico hesitated and then gave a sigh. 'You're right, of course.' He walked over to Abby and hugged her. 'I'm sorry. I don't mean to be overprotective. I just hate seeing you in pain.'

'I love the fact that you're overprotective,' Abby said huskily. 'You think I want a man who doesn't give a damn about me?'

Zan blinked back tears and went to call the anaesthetist.

When she came back, Carlo had already set up an intravenous infusion.

'Let's give her 500 mils of Hartmann's solution,' he

instructed, and Zan did as he asked, attaching the giving set to the bag and hanging it from the pole.

'Why do I need that?'

Abby was looking slightly nervous but Carlo was quick to reassure her.

'An epidural can drop your blood pressure so we put up a drip to prevent that happening.'

Half an hour later Abby was sitting up and smiling, the pain a distant memory.

'This is like magic!'

Nico was looking slightly more relaxed. 'It was a good idea. I should have let you have it sooner.'

'We wouldn't have given it much earlier,' Zan told him, 'because it can switch off the contractions. The cervix has to be more than three centimetres dilated.'

She checked Abby's pulse, blood pressure and breathing, as well as monitoring her contractions and the foetal heart.

'Can you check every fifteen minutes?' The anaesthetist gave her some instructions and talked to her about topping up the epidural.

Carlo was checking the foetal heart. 'The baby is doing fine,' he said quietly.

Nico raked a hand through his hair. 'So what happens now?'

'We wait,' Carlo said. 'But don't expect this to be quick.'

Abby sighed. 'I feel guilty. You two should be at home, celebrating Christmas.'

Remembering how special Christmas Eve had been, Zan briefly met Carlo's eyes and then looked away.

Was it too late for them?

Did she trust him?

She was suddenly frustrated that they were surrounded by people. She didn't know when she was going to get the chance to talk to him again. She didn't know what his plans were.

And why was he still at the hospital when those men were on the loose?

Carlo seemed unconcerned, concentrating his attention on Abby and the baby, checking the foetal heart-rate with each contraction.

'The baby seems fine but your bladder isn't emptying properly,' Zan said, having examined Abby again. 'We need to put a catheter in.'

Abby pulled a face. 'That didn't happen to me when I had Rosa.'

Carlo gave a rueful smile. 'This baby is in a different position, I'm afraid.'

Zan washed her hands and fetched a catheter pack, aware that Nico was looking more and more tense.

By contrast Carlo was relaxed and in control, nothing about his manner betraying his concern. In fact, Zan was surprised that he hadn't interfered more, but he seemed content to let her manage the labour.

They made Abby more comfortable and continued to stay with her. Nico left once more to get some coffee and breathe some fresh air, but apart from that he was by his wife's side for the whole time.

It was growing dark outside when Abby screwed up her face. 'I want to push.'

Zan examined her again and shook her head. 'Not yet. You're not fully dilated.'

Abby gave a sob. 'So why do I have the need to push?'

'Because of the way the baby is lying,' Carlo said quietly, sitting on the side of the bed and taking her hand. 'If you push now you will bruise your cervix.'

They helped Abby to breathe gently, encouraging her not to push, and then finally Zan was satisfied that the cervix was fully dilated.

Nico looked at Carlo, his jaw tense. 'At what point do you operate?'

Carlo smiled and put a hand on his shoulder. 'She's doing very well. I have no intention of operating.'

'But?'

Carlo shook his head, his expression exasperated. 'Have I ever told you that you make a very bad relative?'

Nico sucked in a breath and paced across the room. 'You wait until you're in this position.'

Zan felt a shaft of pain shoot through her. She didn't want to think of Carlo having children with anyone but her. He'd be a great father.

Suddenly aware that he was looking at her with a keen expression on his face, she dropped her eyes and forced her attention back to the job at hand.

'I can see the head,' she said quietly. 'The baby's rotated well so you shouldn't have any problems.'

She opened the delivery pack and got everything ready, then helped move Abby into a more comfortable position.

'I want to go home now,' Abby groaned. 'I've had enough.'

Nico slipped an arm around Abby's shoulders and looked at Zan. 'How much longer?'

'Not long, but babies tend to do things at their own pace.'

'I don't know how you do this every day.' Nico ran a hand through his hair and shook his head. 'I couldn't stand the stress.'

'The stress is because you're the father,' Carlo pointed out, his eyes flickering to the monitor to check on the baby's heart-rate. 'Believe me, it's different when you're the doctor.'

'I never realised how helpless it feels to be the patient,' Nico muttered, dragging both hands through his hair. 'I'm never going to be unsympathetic again.'

'You're the most sympathetic doctor I know,' Abby said, touching his face lovingly, her face drawn and tired from pushing. 'And I love you.'

Nico gave a groan and bent to kiss her. 'I love you too, *tesoro*. More than life.'

Envying their close relationship, Zan concentrated on delivering the head, aware that Carlo was watching her closely.

She was grateful that he was there. It was a far from straightforward delivery and if she had problems she had every confidence that he would be able to solve them.

She checked that the cord wasn't around the neck and then waited for the next contraction to deliver the shoulders.

'Little boy, Abby,' she said gruffly, as the baby slithered into her hands. She lifted him onto Abby's stomach.

'A boy?' Nico couldn't hide his delight and Carlo gave him a hug.

'Congratulations.'

An hour later Abby and the baby were washed and installed comfortably in bed, so Zan slipped up to the SCBU to look at Eddie.

Kelly was sitting by the side of a normal cot, gazing wistfully at the sleeping child.

Zan tiptoed up to her, delighted to see that Eddie was no longer in the intensive-care cot. 'They've taken him out of the incubator?'

Kelly nodded. 'Apparently he's doing a lot better. His brain scan was normal and his breathing is good, although they're still having to watch his sats, whatever that means.'

Zan smiled. 'It's medical-speak for the amount of oxygen in the blood.'

'Oh, right.' Kelly gave her a grateful smile. 'And they're

still tube-feeding him, although we're giving him a go at breast-feeding every time he has a feed.'

'Well done.'

Zan turned to see Mike coming up behind them, his arms full of soft toys, a huge smile on his face.

'How is he?'

'He's great.' Kelly smiled at him and Zan was relieved and delighted to see them so happy together.

The death of Mike's brother had obviously been the cause of many problems between the couple. It was fortunate that things with the baby had turned out so well.

She wished them goodnight and then glanced at her watch. Time to go back to Kim's.

On the way past the nurses' station she stopped and spoke to the sister.

'Eddie is doing well.'

The sister nodded. 'Unbelievably well.' She gave a gentle smile and looked across at the couple who were bent over the cot. 'Nice to have a happy story at Christmas.'

Zan walked back to the staffroom, pulled on her coat and made her way down the stairs to the front of the hospital. A huge Christmas tree dominated the foyer and she looked at it briefly, wondering why Christmas Eve seemed so long ago.

She was longing to go home, but as they still hadn't caught the men who were threatening Carlo she wasn't allowed to.

She slipped a hand into her pocket to check that she still had Kim's keys safe and then pushed through the revolving doors and into the cold night air.

Lights exploded in her face and she blinked and lifted a hand to shield her eyes, trying to work out what was happening.

A group of people swarmed around her, most of them with cameras, some with recording equipment. There was a furious sound of camera shutters and blinding flashes and suddenly everyone seemed to be calling her name, jostling for her attention.

'Miss Wilde?'

How did they know who she was?

Bemused by the attention, she backed away slightly but they closed in tightly, pelting her with questions before she could escape.

'Is it true that you're having a relationship with Carlo Santini?'

'Did you see the men that broke into your flat?'

Zan looked round, desperate for some help, but there was no one around. How had this gaggle of press managed to congregate outside the hospital without anyone noticing?

One reporter, a small man with a nasty expression on his face, elbowed his way past the others. 'Is it true that they're after him because he let a baby die?'

Outrage exploded inside her. 'Mr Santini is the best obstetrician I've ever worked with,' she said, her voice shaking. 'There are all sorts of reasons why babies are stillborn but I know that Carlo wasn't responsible for that death.'

'How long have you known him?'

The questions came all at once and she shook her head, looking for an escape.

Poor Carlo.

If this was the sort of hassle that he encountered then no wonder he found it hard to lead a normal life.

Another reporter wriggled to the front of the crowd. 'Did you know that a woman in Italy has filed a paternity suit against Carlo?'

Zan froze.

Carlo had a child?

For a moment she felt numb, and then snatches of conversation came back to her.

The press print something different about me almost every day. Some of it is total fabrication, and some of it comes from people with a grudge.

And she remembered what he'd said to her the first night they'd met. *No wife. No kids.*

They might have heard the rumours but she knew Carlo well enough to know that he wouldn't lie to her about that.

She lifted her chin. 'Carlo Santini doesn't have a child.'

They all started shouting questions and another journalist waved something under her nose. 'Don't you read newspapers? It's been in the Italian press for months.'

'I'm not interested in what you print in your newspapers,' Zan said quietly. 'I'm only interested in what Carlo tells me.'

She broke off as she realised what she'd just said. *What Carlo tells me.*

'And you trust him?' The journalist gave her an incredulous look and Zan smiled.

'Oh, yes, I trust him. I trust him completely.'

It had just taken some wild accusations to make her realise the truth.

Abby was right. His name didn't matter.

She'd spent time with the man himself and she *knew* him. Knew him well enough to know that he wasn't guilty of what these people were accusing him of.

She didn't need to hear him tell her because she loved him. She loved him with all her heart. And now she needed to try and find him so that she could tell him to his face.

Hoping that he hadn't left the hospital, she pushed through the pack of journalists and sprinted up the emergency stairs to the labour ward.

One of the midwives was sitting at the desk, sorting out notes.

Zan paused, flushed and breathless. 'Has Carlo gone?'

Suddenly she was desperate to see him.

The midwife looked up, surprised. 'Oh, there you are—I thought you'd gone. I had a call from him five minutes ago. He said to tell you that he'd see you at your flat.'

Zan frowned briefly. Surely he'd told her to stay away from her flat?

There'd obviously been a new development.

Relieved and excited, longing for the opportunity to tell him how much she loved him, she sprinted back down the stairs and took the back way out of the hospital to avoid the journalists.

Carlo gave his nephew a final cuddle and handed him back to Abby.

'He's totally beautiful.'

Abby beamed at him. 'Time you had one of your own.'

Carlo's mouth twisted. 'I don't get that lucky.'

Abby stretched out a hand. 'She loves you, Carlo.'

'Does she?' Carlo's expression was bleak and he glanced up with a frown as Nico flicked through a series of channels on the television. 'Hold it!' He snatched his hand away from Abby's, his voice ragged. 'Go back one!'

Nico did as he'd been instructed and all three of them watched in silence as the television cameras zoomed in close to Zan's shocked face.

Carlo cursed under his breath as he saw her lift her arm as protection against the flash bulbs.

'Where the hell did they come from? And where the hell were the security guys?'

'Hush.' Nico held up a hand and turned up the volume so that they could hear what was being said.

'I'm not interested in what you print in your newspapers,' Zan was saying quietly. 'I'm only interested in what Carlo tells me.'

'And you trust him?' The journalist gave her an incredulous look and Zan smiled.

'Oh, yes, I trust him. I trust him completely.'

Abby gave a womanly smile that bordered on the smug. 'I told you so. I think it's time that the pair of you had a conversation. Don't let her go, Carlo.'

'I don't intend to.' With a brief smile to his brother Carlo strode out of the room and hurried to the labour ward. 'Where's Zan?'

'Oh!' The midwife looked at him in surprise. 'She was here a minute ago and I gave her your message.'

Carlo frowned. 'What message?'

The midwife looked confused. 'You called and left a message that she was to meet you at her flat.'

Carlo felt the blood drain from his face. 'I didn't call.'

'But he sounded Italian and he used your name.' The midwife looked distressed and Carlo shook his head.

'It isn't your fault.' Carlo hit a key on his phone and called Matt, then turned back to the midwife. 'Call the police and tell them to meet me at Zan's flat.'

Without waiting for her answer, he sprinted along the corridor and down the stairs as if he was being chased by demons.

Someone had used his name to lure Zan to the flat and he knew exactly who it was.

And he knew that she was in danger.

Zan went up in the lift, thinking only of Carlo.

What should she say to him?

Was it really possible that they had a future together, despite the differences in their backgrounds?

The lift doors opened and she walked towards her flat, noticing that she had a brand-new door, which was standing half-open.

A light was shining inside, which must mean that Carlo was already there.

She paused on the threshold, slightly uncertain about how she'd feel once she was inside.

The last time she'd walked into her flat all her personal belongings had been strewn over the floor. She hadn't really had time to think about the break-in. All she'd thought about was her relationship with Carlo.

Lifting a hand to touch the solid wood of her new door, she bit her lip. Would it still feel like a safe place to live? Would it still feel like home?

Of course it would.

Zan took a deep breath and pushed open the door, expecting to see Carlo standing in the living room.

It was empty.

'Carlo?'

Her voice sounded tentative and she scolded herself silently. She was behaving like a real wimp.

'Are you in the kitchen?'

She stepped further into the flat, noticing that the Christmas tree was back upright and the whole flat looked completely undisturbed.

She smiled slightly. Everything looked fine. Just like home.

And she didn't feel strange.

She felt safe.

And then she heard the door slam behind her and knew that she wasn't safe at all.

Carlo sprinted out of the hospital straight into the car that Matt had waiting. Journalists swarmed towards them but Matt slammed his foot on the accelerator and they scattered nervously.

'She's at the flat.' Carlo's voice was ragged and he flexed his fingers, preparing for a fight.

Matt kept his eyes on the road. 'I lost her. She didn't go where I expected her to. Fire me.'

'It isn't your fault. This whole situation has been too damned complicated.' Carlo shifted in his seat, anxious to arrive. 'Can't you go any faster?'

Within minutes they shrieked to a halt outside the flats and Carlo was out of the car.

They took the stairs at a run and paused outside the flat to draw breath.

The door to Zan's flat was shut and Carlo flung himself at it, intending to break it down.

'Hold on.' Matt grabbed him before his shoulder made contact and shoved him to one side, reaching into his pocket for a small implement. 'We replaced it with a solid wood door, remember? You'll put your shoulder out. I've got a better way.'

He did something to the lock and within seconds the door swung open.

Carlo stared at him. 'How did you...?'

Matt gave a sheepish grin. 'It's what you pay me for.'

Carlo strode into the flat and stopped dead.

One man lay groaning on the floor. The other had an arm around Zan's neck and a knife at her throat.

She looked at him with relief in her eyes. 'What took you so long?' Her voice was croaky. 'I've used all my moves except the kissing one.'

'Shut up.' The man jerked his arm and Zan gave a cry of pain.

Matt growled angrily and took a step forward, but Carlo held up a hand to stop him. 'No.' He looked at the man, his gaze steady. 'Drop the knife. Now.'

The man replied in Italian. 'I'm going to kill her, Santini. You're about to find out how it feels to lose someone you love.'

'I know that you're hurting,' Carlo said, trying to keep his voice steady, 'and I'm sorry about your baby. But this isn't going to help. Let her go.'

'You should have saved her.' The man's voice was hoarse and his arm tightened around Zan's throat. 'You should have saved my little girl.'

'I'm flattered by your faith in me,' Carlo said, taking a step forward, 'but no one could have saved your child. It's not always possible to find a reason for a stillborn child. Let her go and we can talk about it.'

'Don't come any closer!' The man's eyes were wild and Carlo paused, choosing his words carefully.

'Where's your wife, Signor Agnelli?'

The man breathed heavily. 'At home with her mother.'

'But the person she needs is you.' Carlo held his gaze and moved another step closer, gesturing behind his back for Matt to move to the right. 'She needs you with her. This is something you need to work through together for the sake of the family and there are people who can help you.'

'I shouldn't need to work it through.' The man's voice was ragged. 'I should have a healthy child.'

Carlo nodded, his eyes warm and sympathetic but watchful. So far Zan was being her usual brave self but he saw the fear in her eyes.

He also saw the trust and he felt his gut twist.

She was trusting him to sort it out.

His eyes narrowed slightly, measuring the distance. He still wasn't close enough.

'Everyone should have a healthy child,' he said, taking another step forward, 'but sadly that isn't always the way. However skilled we become at medicine, there will always be unanswered questions. There will always be children who die.'

'You could have saved my baby.'

'No.' Carlo shook his head and moved again, making a final gesture to Matt and praying that he'd understand.

He did.

Matt moved in from the right, providing a distraction, and in that split second Carlo plunged forward and grabbed the hand that held the knife, twisting it away from Zan's throat.

The man snarled in anger and turned on Carlo, hurling his body towards him.

Thrusting Zan out of the way, Carlo sidestepped neatly, but the man regained his balance and came back again, this time aiming for Zan.

With a growl of fury Carlo stepped in front of him and punched him hard, wincing as pain exploded through his hand.

The man staggered slightly and Carlo grabbed him by the throat, powering him against the wall.

'Don't you *ever* threaten a member of my family again!'

Under the relentless pressure of Carlo's fingers the man dropped the knife, his face contorted in pain.

Carlo's muscles bunched as he held the man captive and he said something in Italian, his words making the man blanch.

Matt frowned and took a step forward, prepared to intervene, but Zan's warning shout turned his attention to another threat.

The man on the floor was up on his feet and ready to defend his friend. Zan shouted another warning but Matt was already there.

'I've got him.' With no visible effort he lifted the man off his feet and half carried him to the wall. 'Stand there and shut up. This has got nothing to do with you.'

Carlo turned his attention back to the man he was holding, trying to contain his anger.

'Let him go, Carlo.' Zan was suddenly next to him, her voice soft. 'He needs help. He's devastated.'

'Devastated enough to want to kill a member of my

family.' Carlo's grip tightened and he felt a murderous rage tear through him.

He'd never thought of himself as violent before, but if anything had happened to Zan...

'I'm sorry.' Suddenly all the fight went out of him and the man went limp and started to cry. Great tearing sobs that shook his whole body. 'I don't even know what I'm doing any more. I just wanted to blame someone.'

Carlo's mouth was still tight but he relaxed his grip slightly.

'Of course you did.' Zan reached out a hand, her touch gentle. 'That's a normal part of grieving for someone you love. It's easier to blame someone than believe that something so awful just couldn't be avoided.'

Sensing that the man was no longer a danger to them, Carlo let him go and took a step backwards. Even making allowances for the man's loss, he couldn't be as forgiving as Zan.

The man had threatened his mother, his sister and the woman he loved.

'Nothing will ever take the pain away,' Zan said quietly, 'but time will make it less acute. But Carlo's right—your family needs you. You've already lost a child. Don't lose your family, too.'

Before the man could reply the police stormed into the room and Carlo dragged Zan against him possessively.

He wasn't letting her out of his sight ever again.

He spoke briefly to the police and they handcuffed the two men and marched them out of the door.

Zan watched them go with sadness in her eyes. 'Poor man.'

Matt stared at Carlo. 'The man had a knife to her throat and she thinks he's a poor man.'

Carlo gave a twisted smile. 'I'm afraid I find it hard to be so forgiving.'

Zan sighed and touched his cheek gently. 'I'm not really that forgiving. He frightened the life out of me and he's made your life hell, I know. But he lost a child and grief does odd things to people.' She gave a wan smile. 'I thought you were never going to come. How did you get in?'

'Matt's good with locks.' Carlo moved towards her and she looked at him warily.

'And where did you learn to fight like that?'

Carlo shrugged. 'I always refused to have a bodyguard so Dad made sure I had the right training—a bit like your brothers and your judo, I suppose.'

Her eyes were wide. 'You were scary.'

'I'm Italian. We know how to protect our own and he threatened the most important person in my life,' Carlo said softly.

Matt cleared his throat. 'I'll go and sort things out with the police and ring the family. Nico will want to know that it's all sorted.'

An hour later Zan was curled up on the sofa, snug and warm in Carlo's arms. Judging from the way he was holding her, he was never going to let her go.

And it was a really good feeling.

'Usually all that happens on Boxing Day is that I get to eat the remains of the turkey and the mince pies,' she said lightly, tilting her head so that she could look at him. 'Life with you is certainly exciting; I'll give you that.'

Carlo pulled her against him with a groan. 'When that midwife told me you'd gone to your flat to meet me, I almost had a heart attack.'

'I wasn't thinking straight or I would have realised that it wasn't you,' Zan confessed sheepishly. 'But I was so excited about seeing you that I just dashed off and walked right into their trap.'

Carlo's grip tightened and his eyes darkened in anger. 'They were waiting inside the flat?'

She nodded. 'The moment I walked inside they shut the door and attacked me. I managed to floor one of them.'

Carlo gave a wry smile. 'I wish I could have seen that. I bet you gave him a shock.'

'Well, he hit his head when he fell so I don't think he thought about it too much. Unfortunately the other guy grabbed me from behind and I couldn't shift him. He said he was going to wait until you arrived and then kill me.'

She gave a shudder and Carlo frowned. 'How did he know I was coming?'

'Don't ask me. I can't read men's minds. I just know he wanted to kill me with you watching.'

'Nice guy,' Carlo drawled, and she gave a sad smile.

'Hurt guy.' She let out a breath. 'How did you know I was here?'

'I saw you on television, announcing to the world that you loved me and trusted me,' Carlo said smugly. 'Naturally I tried to find you to compliment you on your taste in men.'

Zan laughed. 'Is your ego as large as your fortune, Mr Santini?'

'Larger,' Carlo said proudly. 'I'm Italian, remember. And size matters when it comes to egos. Egos, Christmas trees and—'

'Yes, yes, I know,' Zan interrupted him quickly, her eyes twinkling and her cheeks pink. 'You still haven't explained how you found me.'

'I asked the midwife where you were. The same midwife who'd told you to meet me at the flat. I put two and two together, as you say in this country.'

'I was starting to get worried.'

Carlo hugged her against him. 'You don't know worried,' he groaned. 'Worried is what I felt when I saw that lunatic holding a knife to your throat.'

She hugged him back and then saw him wince. 'Your hand! I forgot about your hand. Show me.'

Carlo wiggled his fingers. 'I'll live.'

'It's bruising already.' She looked up at him. 'You hit him hard, Carlo.'

She'd never forget the raw fury in his eyes when he'd looked at her attacker and the skill with which he'd freed her. It was no wonder he didn't use a bodyguard.

'He threatened the woman I love.' Carlo's voice was soft and Zan bit her lip shyly.

'You're sure you love me?'

A strange expression crossed his face. 'Could you fetch me some ice for this hand, *tesoro*?'

So his hand was hurting more than he'd let on.

Slightly disappointed that he hadn't declared his love more emphatically, she stood up and hurried into the kitchen.

Maybe he didn't love her that much.

She pulled the ice tray out of the freezer compartment and then gasped.

Inside one of the squares was a stunning diamond ring. *Was he proposing?*

'I love you, Suzannah, and I want you to marry me.' His velvety male tones came from behind her and she turned quickly, still clutching the tray of ice cubes with the ring inside.

'How long has this been in here?'

'Since this morning when we finished tidying up your flat. It's a good job those thugs didn't want ice in their drinks,' he drawled, lifting the ring out of the ice tray and holding it in his palm. It sparkled and winked temptingly and she gazed at it in astonishment.

'You bought it this morning? But it's Boxing Day. You can't buy a ring on Boxing Day. The shops are shut.'

Carlo smiled. 'Not if your name is Santini.'

She shook her head in wonder as he reached forward and took her hand.

'I can't believe you mean this,' she whispered, her lips parting in a sigh as he slipped the ring onto her finger. 'You seriously want me to marry you?'

'Oh, yes.' His dark gaze was fixed on her possessively. 'I've never been more serious about anything in my whole life.'

'B-but you date models and film stars,' she stammered, twisting the ring on her finger and looking at him doubtfully. 'I'm just me.'

'And I love everything about you,' he said softly, pulling her closer. 'I think I loved you from the moment you knocked me onto the wet street. You were brave and funny and dedicated to your patients and you were nothing like the women I've ever known before. I love your green eyes and your dimples and your amazing legs. I love the fact that you care about everyone—I even love the fact that you can give me a black eye if I ever step out of line.'

Zan put a hand on his chest. 'But we're so different. I haven't got money.'

Carlo looked amused. 'But I have more than enough for both of us.'

'Aren't you worried I'd be a threat to your bank balance?'

'Fortunately my bank balance is *big*.' He laughed. 'It would take quite a lot to threaten it.'

Zan looked at him, her eyes twinkling. 'So, if I marry you, do I get to spend your money?'

'You do indeed, *tesoro*.' He was still smiling. 'What did you have in mind?'

'Nothing. I was just teasing.' She looked at him and

smiled shyly. 'I don't care about the money. All I want is you.'

'You're sure?' He sucked in a breath and his arms tightened around her. 'I thought what we had was special but then, after last night, I wasn't sure you felt the same way. I thought I'd blown it totally.'

'I was so angry with you.' She bit her lip guiltily. 'I'm sorry.'

'Don't be.' His voice was gentle. 'You had every right to be angry and, believe me, I felt very bad about not telling you the truth. But everything else about us was real.'

'I know.' She stared into his eyes. 'I realised that when those journalists started spouting lies about you. I suddenly realised just how well I knew you.'

He stroked a thumb over her cheek. 'Do you think what you feel for me is strong enough to withstand the dirt that journalists throw at me?'

'Yes.'

He took a deep breath. 'And how do you feel about living in Italy with me?'

'Excited.'

She couldn't believe that it was really happening. That he really wanted to marry her.

He lowered his head and took her mouth, his kiss hot and demanding, and when they finally broke apart she was flushed and breathless.

'When you were shouting at me last night, you said you didn't want my babies and that you weren't going to punch the woman I married. Frankly, I had trouble keeping up. What did you mean?'

'Oh…' Zan went pink and rubbed her toe on the wooden floor. 'It was a conversation I had with Kim.'

'Which was?'

He wasn't letting her be evasive and she gave a sigh.

'She asked how I'd feel if you married someone else and I said I'd want to punch her on the nose.'

Carlo threw back his head and laughed. 'Good job I'm marrying you, then.' He hesitated slightly and there was an odd gleam in his eye. 'And the baby bit?'

She blushed shyly. 'I looked at you on Christmas Eve when you were Father Christmas and I knew I wanted to have your children.'

His smile faded. 'And do you still feel that way?' His voice was hoarse. 'Do you still want my babies, *tesoro*?'

She sucked in a breath. 'More than anything.'

'And you've forgiven me for keeping my identity a secret?'

'Providing you never keep a secret from me again.' She reached up to kiss him. 'Otherwise I might just give you a black eye.'

He hugged her close. 'No more secrets. I promise you that. From now on we share everything. And you need to stop doing the Lottery. It would be embarrassing if we won.'

Zan smiled. 'I've already won,' she said softly, standing on tiptoe to kiss him. 'I found you.'

The world's bestselling romance series.

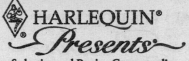

HARLEQUIN®
Presents

Seduction and Passion Guaranteed!

Back by popular demand...

EXPECTING!

She's sexy, successful and PREGNANT!

Relax and enjoy our fabulous series about couples whose passion results in pregnancies... sometimes unexpected!

Share the surprises, emotions, drama and suspense as our parents-to-be come to terms with the prospect of bringing a new life into the world. All will discover that the business of making babies brings with it the most special love of all....

Our next arrival will be

HIS PREGNANCY BARGAIN by *Kim Lawrence*
On sale January 2005, #2441
Don't miss it!

THE BRABANTI BABY by *Catherine Spencer*
On sale February 2005, #2450